What Kids Say About Carole Marsh Mysteries . . .

I love the real locations! Reading the book always makes me want to go and visit them all on our next family vacation. My Mom says maybe, but I can't wait!

One day, I want to be a real kid in one of Ms. Marsh's mystery books. I think it would be fun, and I think I am a real character anyway. I filled out the application and sent it in and am keeping my fingers crossed!

History was not my favorite subject till I starting reading Carole Marsh Mysteries. Ms. Marsh really brings history to life. Also, she leaves room for the scary and fun.

I think Christina is so smart and brave. She is lucky to be in the mystery books because she gets to go to a lot of places. I always wonder just how much of the book is true and what is made up. Trying to figure that out is fun!

Grant is cool and funny! He makes me laugh a lot!!

I like that there are boys and girls in the story of different ages. Some mysteries I outgrow, but I can always find a favorite character to identify with in these books.

They are scary, but not too scary. They are funny. I learn a lot. There is always food which makes me hungry. I feel like I am there.

What Parents and Teachers Say About Carole Marsh Mysteries . . .

I think kids love these books because they have such a wealth of detail. I know I learn a lot reading them! It's an engaging way to look at the history of any place or event. I always say I'm only going to read one chapter to the kids, but that never happens–it's always two or three, at least!
–Librarian

Reading the mystery and going on the field trip–Scavenger Hunt in hand–was the most fun our class ever had! It really brought the place and its history to life. They loved the real kids characters and all the humor. I loved seeing them learn that reading is an experience to enjoy!
–4th grade teacher

Carole Marsh is really on to something with these unique mysteries. They are so clever; kids want to read them all. The Teacher's Guides are chock full of activities, recipes, and additional fascinating information. My kids thought I was an expert on the subject–and with this tool, I felt like it!
–3rd grade teacher

My students loved writing their own Real Kids/Real Places mystery book! Ms. Marsh's reproducible guidelines are a real jewel. They learned about copyright and more & ended up with their own book they were so proud of!
–Reading/Writing Teacher

"The kids seem very realistic–my children seemed to relate to the characters. Also, it is educational by expanding their knowledge about the famous places in the books."

"They are what children like: mysteries and adventures with children they can relate to."

"Encourages reading for pleasure."

"This series is great. It can be used for reluctant readers, and as a history supplement."

The Mystery at JAMESTOWN

FIRST PERMANENT ENGLISH COLONY IN AMERICA!

by

Carole Marsh

First Edition

Published by Gallopade International/Carole Marsh Books. Printed in the United States of America.

Managing Editor: Sherry Moss
Cover Design: Michele Winkelman
Picture Credits: Mike Yother, Hoodie-Hoo Studios
Content Design: Steven St. Laurent, Line Creek Creative

Bloodhound picture compliments of Dick and Sherry Duling of Sherick's Bloodhounds, Quenemo, KS.

The cover photograph is a depiction of Jamestown Settlement's *Susan Constant* and *Godspeed,* recreations of two of the three ships that brought America's first permanent English colonists to Virginia in 1607.

Gallopade would like to acknowledge the APVA at Historic Jamestowne and the Jamestown Yorktown Foundation for lending us their expertise.

This book is a complete work of fiction. All events are fictionalized, and although the names of real people are used, their characterization in this book is fiction.

Hey, kids! As you see–here we are ready to embark on another of our exciting Carole Marsh Mystery adventures! You know, in "real life," I keep very close tabs on Christina, Grant, and their friends when we travel. However, in the mystery books, they always seem to slip away from Papa and I so that they can try to solve the mystery on their own!

I hope you will go to www.carolemarshmysteries.com and apply to be a character in a future mystery book! Well, The Mystery Girl is all tuned up and ready for "take-off!"

Gotta go... Papa says so! Wonder what I've forgotten this time?

Happy "Armchair Travel" Reading,

Mimi

The Mystery at JAMESTOWN

FIRST PERMANENT ENGLISH COLONY IN AMERICA!

20 Years Ago . . .

As a mother and an author, one of the fondest periods of my life was when I decided to write mystery books for children. At this time (1979) kids were pretty much glued to the TV, something parents and teachers complained about the way they do about video games today.

I decided to set each mystery in a real place–a place kids could go and visit for themselves after reading the book. And I also used real children as characters. Usually a couple of my own children served as characters, and I had no trouble recruiting kids from the book's location to also be characters.

Also, I wanted all the kids–boys and girls of all ages–to participate in solving the mystery. And, I wanted kids to learn something as they read. Something about the history of the location. And I wanted the stories to be funny.

That formula of real+scary+smart+fun served me well. The kids and I had a great time visiting each site and many of the events in the stories actually came out of our experiences there. (For example, we really did stick our toes in the cold ocean, climb Jockey's Ridge, and see *Flyer* for ourselves!)

I love getting letters from teachers and parents who say they read the book with their class or child, then visited the historic site and saw all the places in the mystery for themselves. What's so great about that? What's great is that you and your children have an experience that bonds you together forever. Something you shared. Something you both cared about at the time. Something that crossed all age levels–a good story, a good scare, a good laugh!

20 years later,

Carole Marsh

Christina Yother | **Grant Yother** | **Alex Chapple** | **Courtney La Russo**

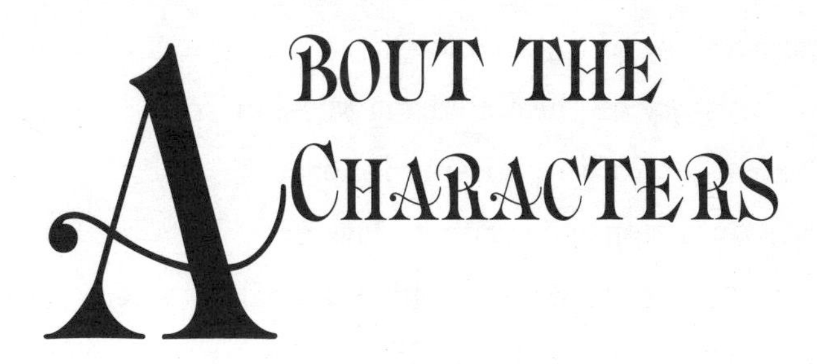

About the Characters

Christina Yother, 10, from Peachtree City, Georgia

Grant Yother, 7, from Peachtree City, Georgia
Christina's brother

Alex Chapple, 8, from Peachtree City, Georgia

Courtney La Russo, 10, from Peachtree City, Georgia

The many places featured in the book actually exist and are worth a visit! Perhaps you could read the book and follow the trail these kids went on during their mysterious adventure!

Titles in the Carole Marsh Mysteries Series

#1	The Mystery of Biltmore House
#2	The Mystery on the Freedom Trail
#3	The Mystery of Blackbeard the Pirate
#4	The Mystery of the Alamo Ghost
#5	The Mystery on the California Mission Trail
#6	The Mystery of the Missing Dinosaurs
#7	The White House Christmas Mystery
#8	The Mystery on Alaska's Iditarod Trail
#9	The Mystery at Kill Devil Hills
#10	The Mystery in New York City
#11	The Mystery at Disney World
#12	The Mystery on the Underground Railroad
#13	The Mystery in the Rocky Mountains
#14	The Mystery on the Mighty Mississippi
#15	The Mystery at the Kentucky Derby
#16	The Ghost of the Grand Canyon
#17	The Mystery at Jamestown

CONTENTS

1 All Wet!

Christina, Grant, Mimi, and Papa had just landed at the airport in Norfolk, Virginia. It was the first day of summer; school was over.

"Let VACATION begin!" Grant, age 7, squealed.

Papa revved the *Mystery Girl's* engines a little and pulled into a hangar. "Let the screaming stop," he pleaded with his grandson.

"Vacation, smaymation," Mimi grumbled. "It's always work work work for me."

Christina, her 10-year-old granddaughter, giggled. "Mimi, your work is your play! You write kid's mystery books. Everywhere we go, you have a good time researching and writing and taking pictures. You know that's true."

Mimi smiled. "Yes, I'm just teasing."

"Well, I'm not," said Papa. "Let's unload gear first, talk second."

"Let's eat first, unload second," Grant suggested, rubbing his tummy.

"Let's all go in the air-conditioned terminal and let someone else unload," begged Christina, wiping her sweaty forehead.

"Let's shop first, second, and third!" suggested Mimi.

Suddenly, the entire family began to laugh. "Nothing silly about us!" said Mimi.

Papa cleared his throat. "Nothing busy, either. I've unloaded everything while all you guys did was yak yak yak."

"Aw, Papa, you figured out our ruse," teased Christina.

Grant looked around. "I don't have a ruse," he disagreed. "I only have a backpack."

The others laughed. Grant frowned. Just because he was the youngest and didn't always catch on to everything over his head right away was no reason for them to laugh at him, he thought. "There's no reason..." he began.

"We know! We know!" the others interrupted.

"We're not laughing at you, Grant," Mimi promised, giving her grandson a big hug. "We're laughing with you."

"Well HA HA!" Grant said. "I'm laughing AT you!"

When the others looked puzzled, Grant pointed behind them. Suddenly a big spray of water hit them! A wash truck was hosing down a nearby plane and the glistening spray arched right over onto Mimi's, Papa's, and Christina's heads. They squealed.

"Feels good and cool," Christina insisted, but her brother did not believe her.

"Messed up my hat!" Mimi groused. She always wore a hat.

"Maybe they could hose down the *Mystery Girl* while they're at it," Papa said hopefully. He hated for his little red and white airplane to get dirty. But the water stopped just as suddenly as it had begun. A young man in khaki pants and vest came running up to them.

"I'm so sorry!" he insisted. "Really! I didn't mean to get you all wet. Are you ok?"

"I am," said Grant, hands on his hips, swaying back and forth smugly.

Christina warned him, "He who laughs last laughs... well, I forget how that saying goes, little brother, but it means beware!"

"These grouchy little varmints are my grandchildren," Papa said. "Don't worry about the water, well, except for the hat maybe?" He gave Mimi a hopeful look.

Mimi grinned and stuck out her hand. "I'm Carole Marsh, and if the only bad thing that happens to me on this trip is that my hat gets wet, well, I can handle that."

The young man looked relieved. He shook hands all around. "Whew!" he said. "I'm so glad I'm not in trouble with you guys. Can I buy you some iced tea or something to make up for the uh, unexpected shower?"

"Sounds like a winner!" said Papa, who never met a

stranger, and they all headed for the terminal.

Lugging their rolling backpacks behind them, Grant and Christina followed the adults.

"Hey, Christina," Grant said, pointing up ahead. "What's all that stuff that guy has hanging from his pants? Is he a mechanic or something?"

Christina walked faster and looked at the gear dangling from the man's belt and cargo shorts' pockets. At first she thought it looked like gardening stuff–a trowel, a measuring tape, a magnifying loupe, and a cloth bag with a drawstring. She looked at the man's long knee socks and chunky shoes. He also wore a pith helmet like people wear in the jungle. For a moment, she was totally perplexed. Then suddenly she snapped her fingers.

"Grant," she said. "I think he's an archaeologist!"

2 Skeletons and a Change of Plans

In the terminal, Christina was wise enough to wait patiently before interrupting the adults who had already settled at a table by the windows and were talking rapidly as if they had known each other forever.

However, Grant just couldn't wait for an answer. "Are you a real archaeologist?" he blurted. The man set down his coffee cup and gave Grant a big grin. With his spiky blond hair, twinkling blue eyes, deep tan, and rosy cheeks, the man really looked like a grown-up Grant to Christina.

"Yes, I am!" he said proudly. "Can you dig it?" That made everyone laugh, although Christina was not really sure Grant got the pun.

"What do you dig?" Grant asked, still curious. He loved anything about dirt. After all, in the dirt was where you found arrowheads, fossils, and dinosaur bones!

The man wagged his head back and forth. "Oh, artifacts like potsherds. And ancient tools. And bricks and bones..."

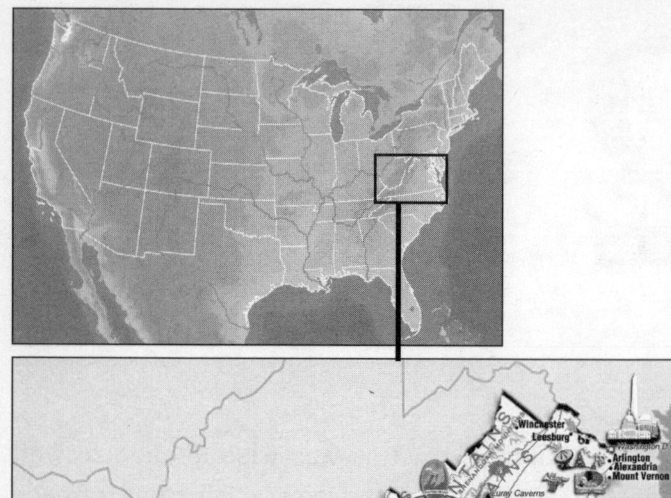

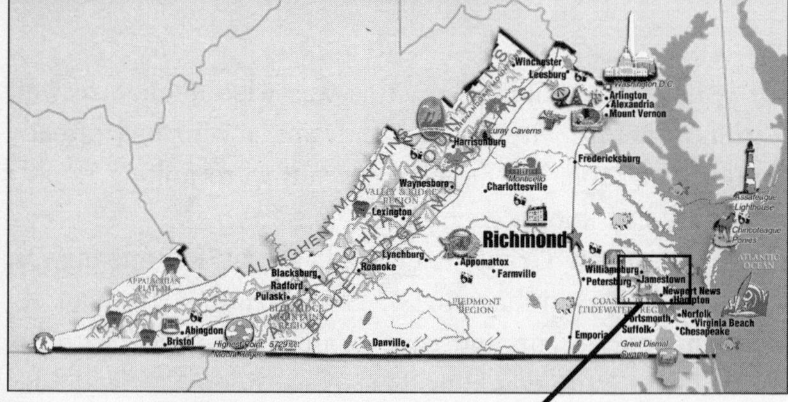

Winchester
Leesburg
Washington D.C.
Arlington
Alexandria
Mount Vernon
Luray Caverns
Harrisonburg
Fredericksburg
Monticello
Waynesboro
Charlottesville
Lexington
ALLEGHENY MOUNTAINS
APPALACHIAN MOUNTAINS
BLUE RIDGE MOUNTAINS
Richmond
Assateague Lighthouse
Chincoteague Ponies
ATLANTIC OCEAN
Lynchburg
Roanoke
Appomattox
Farmville
Blacksburg
Radford
Pulaski
Williamsburg
Jamestown
Petersburg
Newport News
Hampton
PIEDMONT REGION
Norfolk
Virginia Beach
Portsmouth
Suffolk
Chesapeake
Abingdon
Bristol
Danville
Emporia
Great Dismal Swamp

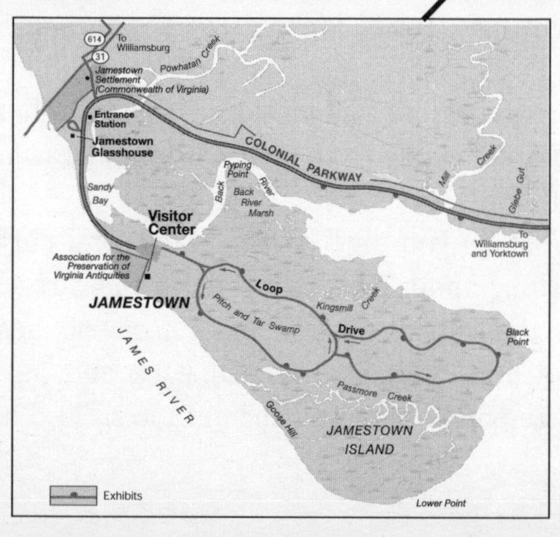

614
31
To Williamsburg
Powhatan Creek
Jamestown Settlement (Commonwealth of Virginia)
Entrance Station
Jamestown Glasshouse
COLONIAL PARKWAY
Mill Creek
Glebe Gut
Pyping Point
Back River
Back River Marsh
Sandy Bay
Visitor Center
To Williamsburg and Yorktown
Association for the Preservation of Virginia Antiquities
JAMESTOWN
Loop Drive
Kingsmill Creek
Pitch and Tar Swamp
Black Point
JAMES RIVER
Passmore Creek
Goose Hill
JAMESTOWN ISLAND
Exhibits
Lower Point

Grant got all excited. "You mean like skeletons?"

Now the man scrunched his shoulders down tight. He leaned forward on his elbows and put his face close to Grant's. "Yes!" he said. "Skeletons!"

"What a cool job!" Grant said, and satisfied with the answer, headed off to the fast food counter to order lemonade.

Christina hung around; she didn't like the sound of this. If Mimi got excited about something like this, if often changed their travel plans. And Mimi could really "dig" skeletons. After all, she wrote mystery books for kids, so ghouls and ghosts and skeletons and mummies and such were right up her writing alley.

"I remember you, Joe!" Mimi said. "We met when you were in charge of a dig on Roanoke Island. Where are you working now?" Mimi asked, as the two shook hands.

Joe waved his arm toward the windows. "The greatest archaeological dig ever!" he said. "Up at Jamestown. It's like a crime scene up there," he added merrily. "Fascinating, just flabbergasting, actually. And we have a new Archaearium...and the 400th anniversary's underway...and so much is going on, I mean wow!"

"Whoa! Whoa!" cried Papa, and Christina giggled. Her grandfather was a pilot and a cowboy and claimed to be Mimi's "trail boss" to keep her on track with her writing projects. "Crime scene? Archaearium?"

Now Christina was so curious that she spoke up.

"Are you talking about the Jamestown we study in school in history? The first English settlement in America?" All this had been on a test recently.

"The first permanent English settlement," Joe corrected her. "As you may know, there was an earlier attempt to establish a colony in the New World...south at Roanoke Island, North Carolina."

"Oh, I know that one," Christina said proudly. "The Lost Colony! We went to the outdoor drama about it when Mimi was working on a mystery about Blackbeard the Pirate. That's where Virginia Dare was born, but all the colonists vanished–right?–leaving no trace but a sign that said something like CROATAN."

"Good job!" said Joe, and Mimi and Papa beamed proudly at their granddaughter. "And we still aren't sure what happened to those men, women and children. It's a mystery!"

"And what about the *Nina*, *Pinta*, and *Santa Maria*, and Plymouth Rock, up in Massachusetts?" Mimi asked. Christina knew Mimi was just trying to get a history lesson given here; she didn't fool her!

"That colony was established more for religious freedom reasons," Joe explained.

"So what about JAMESTOWN?" Papa asked impatiently.

Joe cleared his throat. "The Jamestown colony was different. It was established to be a permanent foothold in the New World. The men and boys who came were given the goal to set up a real town and figure out ways to make money and discover crops or other things of value that could be exported back to England."

"Only men and boys?" Christina asked, disappointed.

"That's all that came over on the *Godspeed*, *Discovery*, and *Susan Constant*," said Joe. "But don't forget about Pocahontas!"

"That's right!" said Mimi. "What a tale that is!"

"And CRIME SCENE?" Papa asked, still trying to get his original questions answered.

Joe shook his head seriously. "Oh my goodness," he said. "It wasn't a pretty picture. Can you just imagine landing in an unknown place, meeting people you believed were savages, and not having much of a clue as to how you were going to keep from starving to death, much less get along with one another...well, it's a long story, but yes, it leads to some very suspicious skeletal remains."

"Wow!" said Grant, who had walked up with two lemonades in time to hear the story. "I want to know more."

"Me too!" Mimi squealed with an eager look at Papa.

Christina groaned. "We were going to Busch Gardens," she reminded them. In her imagination, she saw the fun water rides and rollercoasters vanishing like a dream.

Sure enough, Mimi said, "Joe, are you headed to Jamestown now?"

"You bet!" said Joe. "Why don't you guys follow me and I'll give you an A-plus tour you won't forget! Besides, you need to see the new Archaearium."

"Ok, ok?" Mimi asked her family. "And then we'll go to the theme park; promise!"

"IT'S A DEAL!" Papa shouted, eager to be off to somewhere. He didn't like to stay in one place too long.

As the adults headed to get luggage and cars, Christina and Grant sat forlornly at the table, sipping on their lemonade.

"You and your big mouth," Christina grumbled to her brother.

"Sorry," he said. Then he smiled. "But Christina, there are skeletons!"

"Skeletons schmeletons!" she moaned. "I feel a mystery coming on–not a vacation!"

3 Who is James? Where is His Town?

In just a few minutes, Papa had their rental car loaded with luggage. Joe drove up in a rugged-looking jeep with mud plastered all over it.

Grant couldn't resist: "Can I ride with Joe? PLEASE!" Mimi looked at Papa and Papa looked at Mimi and they nodded "ok" to Grant.

Joe led the way out of the parking lot and Mimi, Papa, and Christina followed in the little red convertible (Mimi's favorite car) Papa had rented. It was not far to Jamestown. Of course, Grant–who had not studied this part of American history yet–had asked, "Who is James? Where is his town?"

Everyone had laughed at him good-naturedly. But, really, in the car, Christina, who thought she knew the story of Jamestown, was surprised at the difference in what Joe had described versus what she had learned in school.

"You have to understand," Mimi explained, "that the story of the founding of the colony at Jamestown is a very dramatic story. No one knew exactly what they were getting into. It was a serious journey and needed to be successful if the English were going to gain a strong foothold in what would one day become America."

"So it wasn't America yet?" Christina asked.

"Oh, no," said Mimi. "It was untamed wilderness! The Indians had learned how to live here successfully. But there were many tribes and they sometimes fought with one another. They were not especially happy to see funny-looking newcomers make an appearance and act like they owned everything."

Christina thought about that. "I can see their point of view," she admitted. "But why did you say they were funny-looking?"

Mimi laughed. "Well, just picture it! Here are native peoples accustomed to living in a land that is hot in the summer, filled with mosquitoes and other biting bugs, and so they dress in very few clothes and cake mud on themselves to keep those bugs from biting. And then here come men and boys from across the sea in boats, and they wear thick, heavy clothes. And they don't seem to know about fishing or farming. In fact, all they seem to be interested in is finding gold or other riches or some secret passage to the Orient."

"They didn't know their geography very well," marveled Christina.

"No, they didn't," said Mimi. "After all, it was the so-called New World, and little of it had been explored and mapped."

"And so what happened next?" asked Christina.

"Murder and mayhem! Starvation and tragedy! Deadly diseases! And so much more!" Mimi said dramatically.

Christina sat in the back seat and thought about all this. She had just thought the story of the founding of Jamestown was a sweet little story of the Indian princess girl, Pocahontas, saving the life of Captain John Smith, and everyone living happily-ever-after.

In the meantime, in Joe's Jeep, Grant was learning a thing or two himself. But it wasn't because Joe was talking to Grant. It was because Joe was on his cell phone talking to other archaeologists in Jamestown. This is what Grant overheard:

"Stolen?! They stole artifacts? Skeletal remains? I don't believe it!" Joe was screaming into the phone as he drove down the highway. Mimi and Papa didn't believe in talking on a cell phone while you were driving, so this all made Grant a little nervous.

"Who? Why?!" Joe squealed into his phone. He was very upset. Finally, he slammed the cell phone down and looked around at Grant. "Grant," he said, "when we get to Jamestown, you're going to see that we have a real mystery on our hands!"

Grant nodded seriously, but inside he smiled a secret smile. "A mystery," he told Joe the archaeologist, "is right up Mimi's alley!" And to himself, Grant thought, AND WE ALWAYS HELP HER SOLVE THEM!

4 Jamestown, Unsettled

It was not a good time for a mystery. It was summer and Jamestown, Virginia was in the middle of its celebration of the founding of the first permanent English settlement in what would later become the new nation of America. Tourists were everywhere! There was lots of celebration going on, but not among the archaeologists who were very angry that some of their most important findings had been stolen from the new Archaearium exhibit.

So when they got there, Joe had to run off and tend to important business. He left Mimi, Papa, Grant, and Christina with a very pretty and nice young woman in charge of publicity named Amy.

"I'll give you a special tour!" she promised them. But Mimi and Papa didn't like crowds. They asked if they could just go to the café and enjoy some iced tea for awhile. Amy nodded. She looked at Grant and Christina. "I'm also giving a tour to two VIP kids. Is it ok if we all go together?" The girl seemed very pressed for time. "The boy's name is Alex; he's one of the archaeologist's kids.

And the girl's name is Courtney. She's part Indian. They're about your age."

Christina and Grant exchanged glances. "Sure!' they eagerly agreed. They'd much rather go on the VIP tour with a couple of other kids than with their grandparents, who were always asking boring questions with long answers.

Amy looked relieved. "Then stay right here," she said. "I'll go and get them and be right back!"

As Grant and Christina waited, they wandered around the museum and gift shop area.

"Four hundred years ago is a long time," Grant said.

"It sure is," Christina agreed. "Just think, back then there were castles and queens in England." She pointed to a large portrait of Queen Elizabeth I on the wall. The woman wore an elaborate brocade dress with a butterfly-like collar rising up around her head and fancy hairdo.

"And knights and pirates, too!" Grant added. He looked up at an exhibit about Spanish treasure ships. Both he and his sister admired the gold doubloons and silver pieces of eight. Mimi wore a real-life "piece of eight" around her neck and had showed them how, back then, people snipped little pie-shaped wedges from the coins to pay for goods they bought.

Before they could explore the museum any further, two kids rushed up behind them and surprised them by tapping them on the shoulders. Grant and Christina spun around.

"Are you Grant?" asked a red-headed, freckle-faced boy. "I'm Alex!" He and Grant shook hands.

"I'll bet you're Christina?" a girl with long, blond hair asked. "I am Courtney."

"You don't look like an Indian," blurted Grant.

"Grant!" Christina cried. "Don't be so rude!"

Courtney laughed. "It's ok, Christina. Lots of people think that just because you have ancestors who were Native Americans, you will be dark-skinned and have dark hair in braids. As you can see, however, that's just not true."

"When the colonists first came to Jamestown, they even thought the Indians dyed their skin," Alex shared. "They thought you could rub the stuff off."

"That's silly!" said Grant with a giggle.

"Yeah, but when things are new to you, you often draw the wrong conclusions," Courtney reminded them.

Christina sighed. "Well what conclusions do you two draw about all this mysterious skeleton stealing–right here at Jamestown under the archaeologists' noses...and right in the middle of this special celebration when I'm sure everyone wants everything to be just perfect?"

Alex and Courtney shook their heads. "We don't know what to make of it. Everyone's real upset, but they're trying to keep it all hush-hush, even while they investigate the thefts," said Courtney.

"We're supposed to stay out of the way," Alex added. "But we like to solve mysteries!"

"You, too?!" cried Grant and Christina together.

"Then we should get along fine," Christina added.

"We know your grandmother's a mystery book writer," said Courtney. "We've read some of her books in school. She should write one about this!"

"Hush your mouth!" said Christina with a frown.

"Why?" Alex asked.

"Because," said Christina. "If Mimi gets too interested in what's going on at Jamestown, we'll never get to go ride rollercoasters and stuff. Our entire vacation will be spent right here."

Grant frowned. "And that would be a tragedy," he said seriously.

Alex and Courtney both giggled, but Grant and Christina could not understand what was so funny.

"Aw, there's lots more to do around this part of Virginia than ride rides," said Courtney. "You need to go to Historic Williamsburg and to Yorktown before you leave. They're both very interesting."

"Yeah," Alex agreed. "Williamsburg was the colonial capital of Virginia and it has a bunch of cool buildings and people reenacting life like it was back then. And Yorktown was where the Revolutionary War ended in a big, giant battle."

"Well, I'm allergic to anything that has the word 'Historic' in front of it," grumbled Grant. "And Christina's allergic to anything about battles and war."

Courtney and Alex exchanged glances. "Hmm," said Courtney. "Then you didn't grow up in Virginia, which is all about history and battles–really exciting stuff. I hope we can change your minds."

"I know I can!" said Alex. "I know all the cool, historic, blood and guts facts we kids like to hear. I'll tell you as we go along."

"Along where?" asked Grant.

Suddenly a voice spoke behind them. "Along our tour!" said Amy. "I'm ready, if you kids are?"

The kids nodded. Christina hoped a VIP tour included snacks and gifts, or something.

Little could she know that their tour would include tricks, mistaken identity, clues, and mystery galore!

5 A VIP Tour

Amy began their tour right away by saying, "In the year 1607, the Powhatan Indians were busy with their daily chores, when they were surprised to see three ships come sailing up the James River! The three ships were named the *Susan Constant*, the *Godspeed*, and *Discovery*. They had been sent from England by a group called the Virginia Company.

"The Virginia Company was a group of men, who had a royal charter from King James I of England. The men put up the money to send 104 men and boys to try to establish a permanent English colony here.

"They had many urgent reasons to do this. First, they wanted to claim land for England before the countries of France, Spain, and Portugal beat them to it. Second, they hoped to find riches here to send back to England. Third, they thought they could find the so-called Northwest Passage that would take them on to the Orient. Finally, some English missionaries were eager to convert the Indians to their religion," Amy finished.

"And they did all that?" Christina asked.

Amy laughed. "Not quite! First, they had to try to make friends with the Indians and keep from starving to death!"

Just as the kids started to ask more questions, Amy's walkie-talkie squawked. She pressed the LISTEN button with a worried frown. Quickly, she listened, frowned, and nodded. She pressed the TALK button and said, "I'll be right there!" She turned to the kids and said, "Sorry, but I've got to interrupt our tour for a little while. You kids stay right here and I'll be back shortly." She ran off in a great hurry.

"Did you hear that guy on the walkie-talkie?" Alex said.

"Yeah," said Grant. "He said it was an EMERGENCY. That more of the STUFF was gone. That they had a LEAD."

"Well, I guess we know what he was talking about, don't you think?" said Alex.

"You mean more skeletons have gone missing?" asked Christina.

"Oh, it's not just skeletal remains that are of priceless value here at Jamestown," Courtney explained. "Any artifacts are. This is not just Jamestown's history... it's America's history!"

"Well, what are we waiting for?" asked Grant. He struck a pose like he was about to sprint off down the path.

"We're waiting for Amy," his sister reminded him.

Grant shook his head. "Negatory," he said. "I'm not

What are we waiting for!?

waiting on anyone or anything. If America's history is going missing, it's my history too since I'm an American. So I'm gonna go find it. Anybody want to join me?"

The other three kids nodded eagerly.

"Where do we begin?" Christina asked.

"I have an idea," Alex suggested. "Why not start at the SCENE OF THE CRIME?!"

6 The Scene of the Crime

The four kids headed immediately to Jamestown's new Archaearium.

"*Archaearium* is a made-up word," Courtney surprised them by saying, as they scampered along the paths, dodging tourists. "And it has a made-up definition, which is 'a place of origin'."

Christina laughed. "That sounds like something Mimi would do–make up a word. But what is an ar-KEE-air-ee-um?" she asked, trying to get the pronunciation right.

"It's this!" said Alex, waving his arm at a new building built over a very old site–a 400-year-old site, to be precise.

"What's inside?" Grant asked.

"Follow me and I'll show you!" Alex said, and the kids hurried up a ramp into the unusual building made of copper and glass.

Inside, Grant and Christina were surprised by two things. One was that the building housed an actual archaeological dig "in progress." And the other was that

Joe was down on hands and knees busy examining an artifact in the dirt.

"Hey, Joe!" cried Grant, as if they were old friends. "We found you! What have you found?"

Joe looked up and grinned. With a grimace, he stood up and brushed dirt off his knees. He walked over to where the children stood above the dig. "Hi, you guys!" he said. "Hi, son," he added with a nod to Alex.

"Hey!" said Grant. "He called you his son!"

Alex giggled. "Well, why not–he's my dad."

"Your dad's *this* archaeologist?" Grant marveled. "I didn't know."

"Sorry, Grant," Joe said. "I guess I forgot to tell you about my son Alex on the ride up to Jamestown in the Jeep."

"No wonder you know so much about this place," Christina said, impressed. Alex blushed.

"We both hang around here a lot," Courtney explained. "In case you didn't figure it out, Amy's my big sister."

"Wow!" said Grant. "Our family affair meets your family affair–cool."

"So what have you found, Joe?" Grant asked again.

Joe grinned. "Oh, about a million things or so!"

That answer silenced the kids. "Well, the place is 400 years old and we've been digging awhile," Joe explained. "During all this time, we've found everything from pots to weapons, as well as about 80 burial sites. And now we've unearthed part of the original location of James Fort, built by the first Englishmen to come here."

Joe waved his arm around at the site and the many artifacts on display. The kids looked up, down, left, and right, realizing that there was a lot here to see.

Grant stooped down and whispered, "And what about the missing S-K-E-L-E-T-O-N-S?"

"Grant!" Christina said. "I think Joe and everyone else listening knows how to spell skeletons."

"I know that!" Grant grumbled back to his sister. "But Joe says it's all H-U-S-H–H-U-S-H!"

Joe just shook his head. "Uh, why don't you guys follow me to my office and I'll catch you up on the events." He turned and climbed out of the site area and the kids followed close behind, trying to see everything they could on the way.

The archaeologist's office was just a small area behind a wall, but it was cool, with its campstools and drawing board, and pictures of skeletal remains and other artifacts pinned to a burlap wall.

The kids automatically settled on the camp stools in front of Joe's desk and listened intently, as if he were about to tell them a ghost story. And in a way, that's just what it was!

"Well, you know that in 1607, 105 men and boys left England on three ships. One man died on the trip, so only 104 actually arrived here at Historic Jamestowne. All that they built or left behind–including a fort and buried bodies–was assumed to have long since disintegrated in the earth. But a few years ago, a project called Jamestown Discovery was embarked upon–and as I said, we've discovered all manner of things."

"Like skeletons!" Grant said.

Joe nodded. "Yes," he agreed, "but a lot more too, only I know to you kids BONES are a big deal, whether they're dinosaur bones or human bones, so I'll tell you a little about that."

"The good parts, please," Christina egged Joe on. She knew that school-age kids often just heard parts of history. Adults and textbooks often avoided sharing the more gruesome aspects about the past. But Mimi always said that kids should learn the truth about history so that they could learn to draw their own conclusions about facts...and so they could help the bad things not happen again. Christina wasn't sure she understood all that yet, but she knew kids did not like to be deprived of the blood and guts and other interesting stuff that was as much a part of the past as the fancy-schmancy parts.

"Ok," Joe agreed. "Then you probably already know the part from school about how Jamestown is the birthplace of America...how much of our present-day government, laws, customs, language, and beliefs came from these first colonists?"

The kids nodded, eager for Joe to get to the "good part."

"I guess you could say that their nerves were frayed," Joe said. "After all, at first, this was just a small outpost with little defense against the many Indian tribes. The English weren't familiar with the land, the people, the hot weather, the brackish water, the lack of food, and almost everything else. Everyone was actually pretty miserable!"

Christina laughed. "Boy, it wouldn't have taken Mimi but about ten minutes to have turned around and headed back. She says she likes all the comforts of home."

"Well, there weren't many comforts here," Joe said. "And so as everyone argued, and got tireder and madder, and scareder of the Indians and starving, it's possible some bad stuff happened."

"Like murder?" said Grant.

"Let's just say that some of the skeletons we've unearthed have obvious wounds," said Joe. "You know," he added thoughtfully, "this was a hard time in history. And when times are hard, people sometimes act differently than they might under other circumstances. So you had people who were brave or cowards, smart or stupid, helpful or cruel."

"So the English were dumb and greedy and mean?" Christina concluded.

"Oh, no!" said Joe. "The most interesting thing that we've discovered at Historic Jamestowne is actually how industrious they were! After the hard times, they really got their act together. They built a fort and used their many talents. Some were glassblowers or botanists; others were blacksmiths or brickmasons. They learned to grow tobacco and sell it back in England which gave the colony money for further improvements."

"But what about the skeletons?!" pleaded Grant, not even bothering to spell it out this time.

Joe shook his head sadly. "Yeah, those skeletons–they're missing. And the worst thing is that it's beginning to look like an inside job."

"You mean you think one of the archaeologists stole the skeletons?" Courtney said. "That's terrible!"

Once more, Joe shook his head. He looked at his son. "No," he said. "They think this archaeologist stole them. Me."

Grant, Christina, and Courtney turned and looked at Alex. Alex looked at his dad. Then, Alex looked like he might faint!

7 A Trip to the Mail Room

Alex was absolutely speechless. "Dad," he finally squeaked out. "You're no thief!"

The other kids wondered if Alex really, really believed that, or if he was actually asking his father to confirm that he had not stolen the valuable skeletal remains.

"Of course, I didn't steal anything!" Joe said angrily. "But someone is sure making it look like I did. And if the police get enough evidence, then they may arrest me."

Now Alex looked like he could cry.

This made Joe try to be a little more cheerful. "Hey, kids," he said. "I didn't mean to burden you with my problems. It will all turn out all right. In the meantime, how about taking this package for me over to the mail station so it can go out to the lab today."

"Ok!" the kids said eagerly. They were happy to help and they wanted to get out of there so they could talk about this terrible situation.

Grant took the package and shook it a little. It rattled just slightly.

"Hey, be careful with that!" Joe warned.

"Ok," Grant promised. "What's in here?"

Without thinking, Joe said, "Bones." When he saw how the kids looked at him–especially his son, Alex–he just shook his head. "I'm sending them to a lab for tests. Go on and get out of here," he said. "I have work to do."

The kids headed for the mail station. They walked glumly down the path, now paying little attention to the tourists or the beautiful late afternoon sunshine and shadows.

"I'm sure your dad didn't do anything bad," Christina said to Alex. "Don't worry, we'll help get to the bottom of this."

Courtney and Grant nodded in agreement, but Alex just kicked his feet in the dirt and stared at the ground as they walked. Christina figured he was trying to make sense of this new bad news.

"Look," Christina said, still trying to cheer everyone up. "Papa gave me twenty dollars. Let's get this mail delivered and I'll treat everyone to ice cream."

"Thanks," Courtney said. "That would be nice."

"Here's the mail station," Alex said glumly.

The four kids went into the small building. Surprisingly, all the lights were out.

"Are you closed?" Courtney called out. "I think it's too early for them to be closed," she said to the others.

Suddenly from the dark shadows behind a counter, a deep voice yelled at them. "Yes, we're closed! But give me that package and I'll get it out of here today." A hand reached out and grabbed the package of bones right out of Grant's hand. "And if you know what's good for you, you'll take this clue and see if you can find the real bone thief, kids!" The hand thrust a piece of white paper at them. Christina grabbed it. Now the voice yelled, "I said get OUTTA HERE!" The kids turned and ran for their lives.

Back outside, the kids ran as far away from the mail station as they could. Out of breath, they stopped and sat on a wooden bench, breathing hard.

"Well, that was curious!" Christina said.

"It sure was," Courtney agreed. "What was that all about?"

"I guess we might can tell from the note that mean guy gave us?" Grant suggested.

Alex, looking sad and mad now, said, "I think I should read it. After all, it's my dad who is in trouble. Maybe this note is a clue that might help prove his innocence."

Reluctantly, Christina handed over the folded piece of white paper. The others hung over Alex's shoulders eagerly as he unfolded the paper and read:

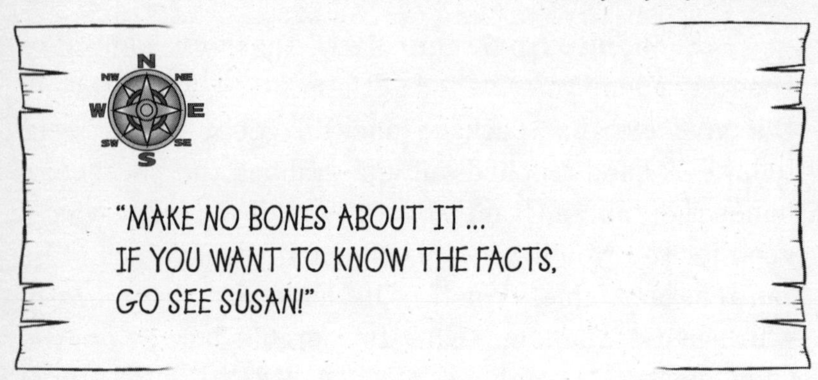

"Are you sure this note is meant for us?" Christina asked. "I don't know a Susan. Maybe the guy at the mail station has us mixed up with someone else."

"I don't think so," said Courtney. "News of the missing skeleton is all the buzz behind the scenes here. I imagine whoever that guy is, he saw that the package was from Joe. Somehow I think he was just waiting to give us this note, although I don't know why."

"Could be a red herring," said Grant.

"What's that?" asked Alex.

"It means a false clue," Christina explained. "Something meant to mislead you."

"Well, I don't have a choice except to hope that this clue is trying to help my dad," Alex insisted hopefully.

"Maybe we should tell your dad," said Grant.

"No way," said Alex. "He's upset enough already. He loves his job at Historic Jamestowne. It would be terrible if he lost it, not to mention losing his reputation."

"I agree," said Courtney. "It's a close-knit community around here. Maybe that guy didn't want us to know who he was, but he wanted to help. I say we explore the clue and see where it leads us."

"Spoken like a true detective!" said Christina with admiration. "I concur."

"Well, I don't understand the need for all the espionage," said Alex, "but I'm ready to try to find the thief on my own."

"I don't know who S.P. Onage is," said Grant, "but we will help you, Alex."

The other kids laughed and Grant looked puzzled. However, Grant often knew he had the last laugh when it came to mystery-solving, so he just shrugged off the teasing.

Christina looked all around. "Well, where is Susan? Is she like Amy, a guide?"

Now, both Alex and Courtney started laughing. Grant joined in, just to get back, but he didn't know what was so funny.

"Susan has got to be the *Susan Constant*," said Alex.

"She's at the dock," added Courtney. "Let's go get this mystery solved!"

8 The *Susan Constant*

The kids headed to Jamestown Settlement (which was in a different location from Historic Jamestowne) where the replicas of the three ships that sailed from England in 1607 were docked. They headed for the ship, the *Susan Constant.*

"Wow," Christina marveled. "It's hard to imagine sailing across the enormous Atlantic Ocean in ships like these."

"It would have been a rough voyage," Courtney agreed. "And taken some time."

"And they didn't have GPS and all that other cool electronic gear boaters have now," said Grant, who loved to boat with Papa on his little red and white boat also named the *Mystery Girl.*

"Believe me, Dad says every step of the Jamestown saga was an adventure," said Alex.

"Let's just remember we're on a mystery adventure," Christina reminded them. "And I don't understand what we're supposed to do next now that we're here at the dock."

Slowly, the kids approached the ship. A man dressed in authentic costume, as Captain Christopher Newport might have dressed, stood high above them on the *Susan Constant*. With a finger, he beckoned the kids to come aboard.

The kids looked at one another, then climbed the gangplank. At the top, a nautical line separated them from the grim-looking captain. Without a word, he handed Alex a folded piece of white paper.

In a deep, commanding voice the captain said, "I think you should read this right away. It was given to me to deliver to four kids who would appear here shortly. I'm sure I have no idea what this is about." The captain turned, as if he had important business below and vanished down into the hold of the ship.

"Well, that was curious, too," said Christina.

Quickly, the kids scampered back down the gangplank and stood in the shade of the ship. Alex looked up at the masts and lines and furled sails and said a special wish that this clue would be more helpful.

"Hurry and read the note," said Courtney.

"The CLUE!" Grant insisted.

"Only if it says something useful," said Alex. He unfolded the note and read:

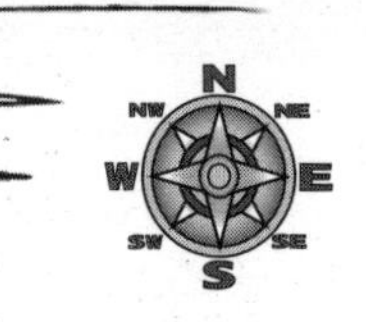

"WHAT ARE YOU DOING HERE?
GO DIRECTLY TO THE INDIAN VILLAGE
TO AWAIT FURTHER INSTRUCTIONS."

Alex stomped his foot. "Well, why did the first clue send us here if we need to be somewhere else?"

"I guess we wouldn't have known that if we hadn't come to the *Susan Constant*," Christina suggested.

"It's getting late in the afternoon," Courtney noted. "If we don't go, the Indian Village will be closed."

"What Indian Village is that?" asked Grant.

"The Powhatan Indian Village, of course!" said Courtney.

9 The Powhatan Indian Village

"By the time the Jamestown colonists got here, the local Powhatan Indians had a well-established chiefdom," Courtney continued, as they hurried to the village. "Almost immediately, there were problems between the natives and the newcomers. For one thing, the English couldn't speak Algonquian, the Indian's language."

"Come on, we'll show you!" said Alex, eager to visit the village before it closed up for the night.

As they entered the replica village, many of the last re-creations of various activities by the costumed interpreters were underway. The kids explored the reed-covered houses, watched Indian women garden or grind corn, and Powhatan children play a game of corncob darts.

In another area, the Indians tanned animal hides, made tools and pottery, and wove natural fibers into cordage. To Christina it was like magically being transported back into history.

"Things seem so peaceful...and productive," she noted aloud, while thinking to herself–until the white men came, when things must have changed dramatically.

Soon, a pretty, young Powhatan girl walked toward them. She held out her hand and said, "Welcome to my village."

"Are you Pocahontas, like in the movies?" Grant asked.

The girl frowned just a little. "That's make-believe," she said. "What you see here is more like how things really were. I represent a Powhatan girl of that era. Let's sit over here in the shade and I'll tell you some things you need to know."

Surprised to get such special attention from such an important person in history, the kids excitedly followed the girl to a clearing in the trees where they all sat criss/cross/applesauce as she began her story.

"By the time the English colonists came to this area, we native peoples had lived here for more than 10,000 years," the girl explained. "Chief Powhatan ruled over more than 32 tribes. The original Indians in this area had been hunters and gatherers. But we Powhatans grew corn, squash, beans, pumpkins, and other vegetables.

"We also caught fish, crabs, and oysters, hunted for wild game, picked berries, and gathered fallen nuts. Everyone worked hard to make our village a good place to live. Women farmed, men hunted, and we kids helped so we would be able to handle such chores when we were older."

When the Indian girl saw how eagerly the children were listening to her, she continued. "Our tribes fought with other tribes sometimes, but we were not prepared for the English to come into our land and try to take over."

"That's what they did?" Christina asked,

"That's what they tried to do," the girl said. "We tried to help the English learn to grow crops. We tried to get along. But sometimes there were misunderstandings, then skirmishes, then outright war! The stronger the English colony grew, the harder it was for the Powhatan people to fight them, especially since the English had guns and other weapons. Pretty soon, most of the Indians died either from war or from diseases the white men had which we had no immunity to. It was all very sad."

For a moment everyone was quiet. It was clear that the Indian girl was letting all this sink in. Finally, Christina asked, "Can you tell us more?"

Much to the kids' surprise, the girl suddenly looked all around, as if checking to see if anyone was watching. In a secretive voice she whispered, "Right now, I need to help you. I was given this note to pass along to you." Quickly, she slipped the note in Christina's hand. Then, to their disappointment, the girl hurried off.

"Come on!" said Alex. "Let's go off into the trees here and read this clue. I don't want anyone watching us."

He led the way and the others followed. Soon, they were in a thicket so gnarled that almost no sunlight penetrated the snarled vines.

They sat on the ground and urged Christina to open the note. When she did, they had to peer into the gloomy light to read:

"WHAT ARE YOU DOING HERE WITH THE ENEMY?
YOU SHOULD BE AT FORT JAMES!
HURRY, BEFORE IT'S TOO LATE!"

The kids looked at one another, stunned.

"What's all this about?" said Alex angrily. "The clue writer sends us one place, then another."

"Maybe we're learning something at each place that the clues take us," Courtney suggested.

"Yeah, but this is urgent," said Grant. "Alex's dad could get in trouble."

"My dad's already in trouble," Alex said. He had not thought about things getting worse, but now he worried that they would. "Come on," he said. "Let's hurry to Fort James."

"But it's almost dark," said Christina. "Mimi and Papa will be looking for us."

"It's not almost dark," noted Grant. "It IS dark!"

"I don't think so," said Courtney, standing up and brushing off the back of her shorts. "I think it's just dark and gloomy here in this thicket. Let's go back to the Indian village."

The rest of the kids got up, but then they all realized that the path had closed in behind them. They did not know which way to go. And, it was indeed dark!

10 A Night In the Forest

By the time they tried several different paths, the kids had scraped their arms and legs on thorns and brambles. They were totally turned around and thoroughly confused.

"I wish we had a compass," said Grant. "Papa always carries a compass." Grant sounded like he could cry.

"I hope Mimi and Papa aren't worried sick," said Christina, who sounded near tears, too. She knew they would be in big trouble if they did not check in with their grandparents right away.

"Amy will look for us," said Courtney. "I think. Unless she went home already."

Alex's voice trembled as he said, "Dad thought I was getting a ride with you, Courtney, like I sometimes do when he has to work late."

As they stood there, frightened and confused, the forest grew even darker and, if possible, more quiet. Grant stepped back on a fallen limb which went CRACK! scaring them all into one big joint jump.

"What was that?" squealed Courtney.

"Just Grant's big feet," said Christina.

Just then there was another loud CRACK!

"That wasn't my big feet," said Grant. Then...

CRACK! CRACK!! CRACK!!! *Something was clearly stomping through the forest toward them.*

11 James Fort

With one great joint gasp, the four children began to run. They each ran as fast as they could, falling, tripping, getting up, and racing helter-skelter out of the forest. Surprisingly, they all ended up in the same clearing where they had begun, where the pretty Indian girl had told them all about Indian life 400 years ago.

Only now, there was no girl. There was no one. They realized that the Powhatan Village had been closed down for the night. They were locked inside! And no one knew where they were.

There was only a little faint light left in the western sky.

"Well, this is a fine Howdy Do," mourned Christina. "I do NOT want to spend the night in these woods. There could be bears, or alligators."

"Or ghosts?" asked Grant, his voice trembling.

"No, silly," said Courtney. "And besides, we don't have to stay in the forest. We'll stay in a *yehakin*."

"The what?" asked Grant, looking all around.

"A house," explained Alex. "See!" He pointed to a

structure shaped like a loaf of bread made of saplings and covered with matted reeds and bark.

"Good idea!" said Christina, heading that way.

"And what will we do for food?" asked Grant, rubbing his tummy.

"We'll look where the women grind corn each day as part of the demonstrations. If we can find some, I know how to make flat cakes of corn meal or maybe some hominy."

"Hominy's made of corn?" Christina asked.

"Sure," said Courtney.

"Hominy hominy does it take to make it?" asked Grant, rubbing his stomach even harder. The others laughed.

"Well, it's good we can laugh," Christina said, "but Mimi and Papa are going to be so worried.

"And so is my dad," added Alex.

"And Amy," agreed Courtney forlornly. "But let's try to do the best we can. Maybe morning will come sooner than we think."

The other kids shrugged their shoulders and dragged their feet in the sand as they slugged toward the house. Christina thought that what you read in history textbooks does not do justice to how things really were. She tried to imagine living in this forest every night, winter and summer.

Sure, you had your friends and family nearby, and surely there was a fire going through the night and the young warriors took turns keeping watch. But how frustrating and scary it must have been, she thought, to always have to

Bears? Alligators? Ghosts of Indians!?

worry about when a warring tribe would attack you, or when the English, whom you could not even understand, might pick a fight, or when a new disease might make the whole village sick and many people die. She shuddered.

In the long house, they found some leftover flat cakes and decided just to nibble on them. They tried to fall asleep on the hides and other bed coverings, but the mosquitoes came along and nibbled on them. It was clearly going to be a long night.

Christina wished that they had made it to Fort James, or even better, back to Mimi and Papa. She was worried about her little brother, who loved to camp, but this was something different.

Just as she continued to list her worries in her head, there was another series of CRACK... CRACK... CCCCCRACKKK!

The other kids bolted straight up, and each one seemed to automatically clasp their hands to their eyes, or ears, or mouth. All except Christina, who listened intently. All she could think of was bears, alligators, or the ghosts of long dead Indians.

As the obviously loud footsteps made their way to the opening of the house, they all held their breaths. Then suddenly, a bright light flashed into their eyes.

"Hoodie Hoo!" cried a deep voice. "Who's that sleeping in the Indians' beds? The three little bears?"

In spite of himself, Grant giggled. "No, it's the four little scared kids," he said.

Into the house stepped a very large and tall man. He was almost invisible in his dark pants and shirt, but the flashlight he held shined enough light to make his star-shaped badge glisten in the night.

"I'm Harry," he said. "The night watchman. Whataya kids doing in here? Got locked in?" He laughed. "Happens all the time!"

Soon, Harry rousted them from their planned sleeping quarters and got them inside the museum gift shop and turned on the lights.

The kids headed for the bathrooms first and the water fountain second. Harry the night watchman waited patiently, pad and pen in hand.

"Names?" he asked firmly, when they all returned.

"Are we in trouble?" Christina asked fearfully. How could they help Alex's dad not get arrested if they got arrested first, she wondered.

"Not with me, you're not," Harry answered. "But Boy, Howdy, I can't say about with your parents, you know."

The kids were quiet. They had a bad feeling that they would certainly be in trouble and grounded or put on restriction or in "time out," or worse–probably for the entire summer, or maybe even the rest of their lives?

Harry took their names and the cell phone numbers of their "next of kin." Then he disappeared into a small office while the kids just stood there and prepared for the worst.

It seemed like he would never come out. And, he didn't before there was a great knocking and banging on the door. Flashlights spun through the night. Shouts of the children's names could be heard. Harry hurried out of the office and opened the door.

"CHRISTINA! GRANT!"

"ALEX!"

"COURTNEY!"

Each child's name was called followed by each child running to the matching "next of kin." But instead of being in trouble, Mimi and Papa, Joe, and Amy seemed tearfully thrilled to see them, and, full of questions.

"What were you thinking?"

"Where have you been?"

"Why didn't you call?"

The kids simultaneously tried to answer all these questions and more all at once, when Harry suddenly blew a loud whistle, startling kids and adults alike into silence.

"Listen up!" he said. "It's after midnight. Maybe you guys should all go home now so I can lock back up. We open again at 9:00 in the morning, if you're interested."

The kids looked at Harry like he was crazy. The adults agreed and grabbed "their" child or children and hauled them out to Jeeps or cars. The kids hardly had a chance to say, "Goodnight," or "See you tomorrow."

And that's what worried Christina as Papa, looking tired, silently drove down the Colonial Parkway to their hotel. Maybe she and Grant would never get to see Alex or Courtney again. Or, get to Fort James and the next clue!

12 Colonial Williamsburg

The next morning, Christina and Grant were especially tired. The night before, they had tried to explain how they got locked in the Powhatan Indian Village. Of course, they left out everything about the clues they had been following...and planned to follow.

But really, Mimi and Papa were just so glad that their grandchildren were safe that they took the explanation gladly. Mimi hugged and kissed them about a million times; Papa sighed a lot. Finally, after stopping at a 24-hour diner for some late-night bacon, eggs, and pancakes, they all had flopped into bed.

Now, there was only one bad thing, but it was a very bad thing. After last night's incident, Mimi and Papa were not about to let Christina and Grant out of their sight today!

"We're going to visit Historic Williamsburg," Mimi said gaily, as if everyone had agreed, which of course they had not.

"But we wanted to see Courtney and Alex today," Grant said.

One look from Papa told him that was just too bad.

"We did promise," Christina tried. But Mimi's "evil eye" stare at her communicated the same thing: You're stuck with grandparents today!

So, the kids decided to make the best of it. What choice did they have? Christina thought that maybe they would learn a little more about Virginia's amazing history, and perhaps some of that might help them figure out the mystery of the missing skeletal remains. Maybe.

The ride to Williamsburg was down the Colonial Parkway, a pretty brick road that ran through a beautiful forest and sometimes beside the water. Papa explained how Jamestown, Williamsburg, and Yorktown were connected in a triangle by the brick road.

"Follow the red brick road," Grant sang in the back seat, trying to cheer himself up.

And since Grant really, really liked to sing, and sing loudly, he followed that up with: "FOLLOW, FOLLOW, FOLLOW, FOLLOW, FOLLOW THE REEEED BRIIIIIIIICK ROAD!"

Mimi was used to Grant's singing shenanigans. "Let's follow quietly, please," she said to her grandson, who then sang, "Follow, follow, follow, follow..." in a tiny baby voice. That made everyone laugh and Christina was glad for everything to sort of be back to normal again.

As they got closer to Williamsburg, Christina grew more excited. Mimi explained to them, "When the English colonists came to Jamestown, they brought the concept of

English law with them. They immediately established a form of government. Later, the government was moved to Colonial Williamsburg."

"Wow!" said Grant. "It seems pretty big and busy."

"Williamsburg is the largest living history museum in America," said Papa, as he parked the car.

After they got their tickets, they headed into the many streets lined with quaint homes and shops that made up Williamsburg.

Christina could not get over how charming the entire village was; she felt like she had gone back in time! The dirt or oyster shell lanes invited them to peek into homes and shops and places as diverse as the blacksmith, the pipemaker's shop, or the wiggery.

They enjoyed the costumed interpreters who explained how candles were made from beeswax, or how sheep were shorn of their wooly coats. Costumed kids pushed wooden hoops with sticks down the lanes.

At lunch, they ate at Christiana Campbell's Tavern. Papa loved the old-timey tavern atmosphere. Mimi admired the pewter place settings. Grant ordered pea soup and Christina ordered Virginia ham and biscuits. Papa ordered calves' tongue! Mimi ordered vegetables, but she was looking eagerly at the dessert tray filled with puddings, cakes, pies, and tarts.

Their waitress wore a long full skirt and apron, and gathered white cap. Some men in the tavern wore fancy breeches, silk waistcoats, and powdered wigs!

After lunch, they shopped for souvenirs. Grant and Papa bought matching tricorn hats. Mimi bought sweet-smelling potpourri, and Christina bought a cornshuck doll.

As the afternoon wore on, Christina began to get worried. She wondered what was going on back in Jamestown. Was Courtney in trouble with Amy? Was Alex in trouble with his dad? And was his dad, Joe, in trouble with the law yet?

Suddenly, Christina had an idea! She had forgotten that she had a cell phone with her in her backpack. Mimi had given it to her to use "only in emergencies." Surely this was enough of an emergency, Christina thought.

When everyone went to the "necessary house"–what the colonial Williamsburgians called the bathroom!–Christina looked up the number for Historic Jamestowne and dialed it. When the receptionist answered, Christina said, "May I speak to Joe the archaeologist, please?"

At first, the woman was deadly silent. In fact, Christina thought she must have hung up on her. Then finally, the woman stammered, "I'm sorry. Joe is unavailable. I mean he is not here. Well, what I really mean to say is...he's been arrested!"

Christina was so stunned that she dropped the cell phone on the ground. A friendly man in a tricorn hat and big, baggy breeches reached down and picked it up and handed it to her.

"Thank you," Christina stammered. The man nodded and strode off on his rounds to light the gaslights. When Christina put the phone back to her ear, she realized that the line was dead; she had been disconnected.

Grant was the first to zoom out of the nearby bathroom and back to the bench where his sister sat.

"Who are you calling?" he demanded. "Mimi said that phone's only for emergencies, you know."

"I know," said Christina in a soft voice. "And it's an emergency all right! I called Joe–he's been arrested!"

Grant's eyes grew big; his mouth fell open. "You mean like in jail? The calaboose? The brig? Stockade? Wow! I never knew anyone who was arrested."

"Grant!" Christina said. "It's not funny. It's Joe, remember? Your friend. Alex's dad. We're supposed to be helping them."

"But we're trapped in Williamsburg," Grant said, sadly. "And we're just kids, so what do we do next?"

As they sat there looking down and out, instead of upbeat about a great vacation treat like visiting Williamsburg, Mimi came out of the bathroom.

"What's wrong?" she asked. "You two look like you just lost your best friend."

Before Christina could stop him, Grant blurted, "We did, Mimi, we...OW! CHRISTINA, WHY DID YOU KICK ME?" Grant grabbed his ankle and made a dramatic squinched-up face of pain.

"Yes, young lady!" Mimi said in surprise, "why did you kick your brother?"

"I didn't mean to, Mimi," Christina promised. "I was trying to get up but my foot slid on the dirt...it was an accident." It was a little white lie, but Christina knew that she and Grant did not want their grandparents to realize that Joe had been arrested.

Suddenly, Grant seemed to figure out what his sister was up to. "Yeah, Mimi," he said, "I think it was just an accident. But I sure am tired. Maybe we could go back to Jamestown now?"

Mimi looked very puzzled. In fact, she looked at her grandchildren with great suspicion. Suddenly, Papa emerged from the bathroom, and having heard the end of their conversation, he said, "No way! I want to go on to Yorktown! I want to see how this history story ends."

Christina groaned then giggled. "Papa, you know how this history ends! We have a revolution and become America, of course."

Papa struck a pose with his hands on his hips. "Are you sure?" he said. "Are you absolutely sure? The last I heard the British are coming! The British are coming! One if by land and two if by sea, and all that jazz. Why, anything could happen! We could win the war or lose! I won't believe the outcome until I see it with the whites of my own eyes," he said.

Mimi laughed, as did some other adults who overheard Papa's dramatic speech. "I think you have a few battles combined there, Papa," she said. "But I agree; we should go to Yorktown tomorrow. We might as well finish this historic triangle now that we've started on it. Then," she added, "we can go to Busch Gardens, like I promised."

"Oh, no!" said Grant. "We don't want to go to Busch Gardens. That's just rollercoasters and rides and other fun stuff."

Christina looked at her brother like he was crazy, then she realized why he was saying all these things. "Yes, yes!" she agreed. "We can always go to a theme park, but we can't always see real historic sites."

Before she could finish her sentence, when she planned to add: "So let's go back to Jamestown tonight"– Papa slapped his thighs. "Good then," he said. "Tomorrow it's Yorktown! Case closed. All is decided." He spun on his heels and headed toward the car.

Mimi did not move. She had her hands on her hips, too. She looked down at her grandchildren with her famous "evil eye" (as Christina and Grant called it) which could always tell when kids were up to something they shouldn't be.

"Something's up," she stated. "And I plan to get to the bottom of it! My grandkids not wanting to ride a rollercoaster? Hmm...very suspicious. Very suspicious, indeed."

"Well, really," began Grant, stirring his foot in the sand, "I would sort of like to ride..."

Suddenly, Christina's foot struck again! Grant grabbed his ankle. Mimi grabbed Christina. "In the car, now!" she said.

Christina sighed. It was going to be a very long night. Especially for Joe, in jail. And, for she and Grant, in trouble. What bad could happen next? She was sure that she didn't want to know.

13 Yorktown Battlefield

"I don't get it," Grant said, as they drove down the Colonial Parkway to Yorktown. "What does Jamestown have to do with Williamsburg have to do with Yorktown?"

In the back seat, Christina put down her crossword puzzle and piped up, "You don't know because you haven't studied that history yet in school."

Mimi, looking fresh and bright all in red and sporting sparkly jewelry this morning, turned around and smiled at her grandchildren. Christina took this as a good sign that maybe she and Grant were out of the doghouse.

"Then why don't you explain it to him," Mimi said to Christina.

"I'll start," said Christina, "but you and Papa may have to pick up the story. I haven't studied it all yet, either." Christina opened the notepad she always had with her and spread it across her and Grant's laps.

"See," she said, drawing a square on the pad. "America's history is sort of like the board games we like to play. First, the English came to Jamestown."

She drew a crown inside the square. "They started up a government with rules and laws right away. But then, after awhile, the Virginia colony was growing and getting stronger and more people were coming over from England. So, they moved the colonial capital up the road to Williamsburg. Right, Mimi?" she asked, just to be sure. When Mimi nodded her blond curls, Christina drew a second square on her notepad with a star in the center of it.

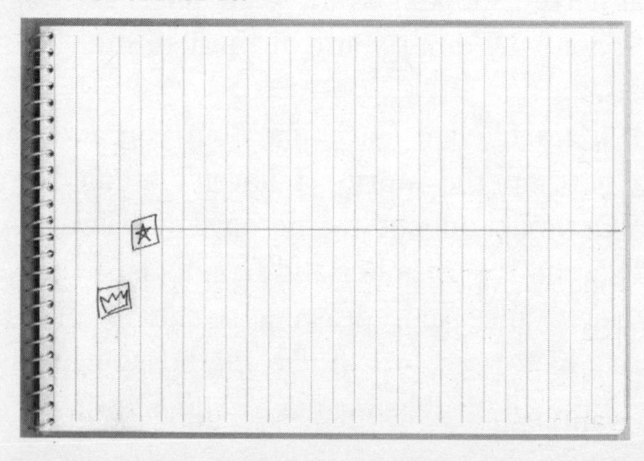

"And then," said Papa, "England began to get the idea that the colonists who had moved here were sort of like young adults who leave for college...they weren't coming back! They wanted to live in this new country and they didn't want to answer to Mom and Dad England, way over there across the Atlantic Ocean."

On her pad, Christina now drew a square way over on the right side of the paper. She put a crown in it and then put an X through the center of it. She smiled as she saw Grant paying close attention to all that was said and all that she drew.

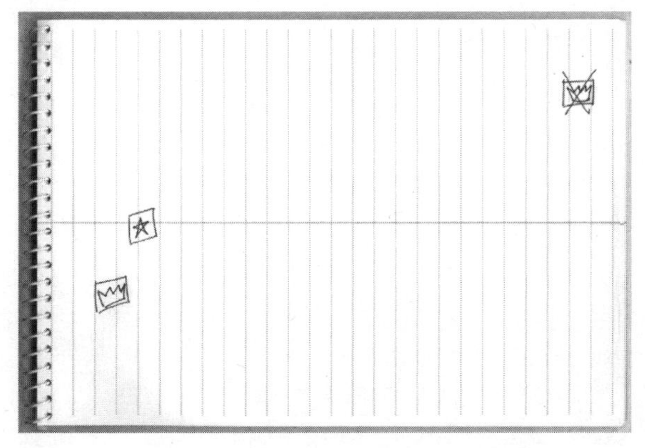

"And then," said Mimi, picking up the story, "there was all out war! The Revolutionary War. The colonists all up and down the east coast wanted to be free. They felt strongly enough about this to fight for their freedom. Even though it was not easy to fight against what had once been their homeland, they believed that they now had a new home."

Grant grinned. "And it was called America?"

"Not yet!" said Mimi. "But after the long, hard, bloody war the English finally had to surrender at Yorktown. And the rest, as they say, is history."

"Yes! There was a Declaration of Independence and George Washington was named president of a whole new country–the United States of America!" said Christina proudly.

On her pad, Christina drew a square with a cannon in the center to represent Yorktown. Then she drew a large square and put an American flag in it.

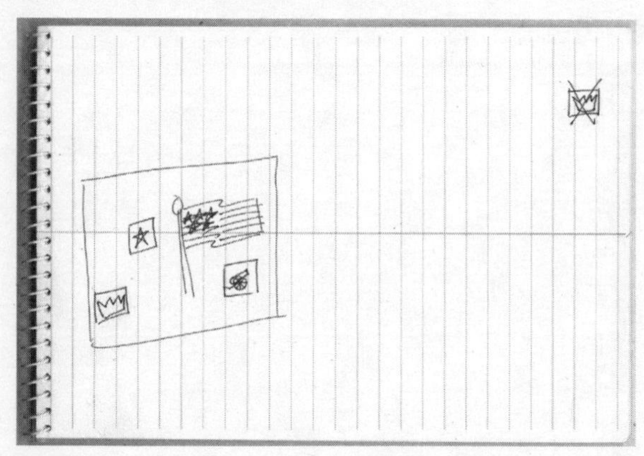

"Well, let's quit talking about this great battle and see where it took place for ourselves," said Papa, pulling into the parking lot.

On the one hand, Christina and Grant were now excited about this all-American story. On the other hand, they were not happy to be delayed from getting back to Jamestown to help Alex and his dad.

Grant took the pen away from Christina and drew a

square on the pad. In the center he drew a "sad face," then over the face drew lines to represent jail cell bars. Christina nodded sadly.

For the next few hours, Christina and Grant completely forgot about the mystery that they were supposed to be pursuing. Yorktown Battlefield and the Yorktown Victory Center were a lot more interesting than they ever imagined.

"Wow!" said Grant, looking at the diagrams in the museum. "This was really a gigantic war. And all those funny-looking guys with weird hair were part of the revolution."

"Who?" asked Mimi, making notes in her research notebook.

Christina giggled. "He means George Washington and Thomas Jefferson and guys like that," she explained.

"Grant!" Mimi admonished, but the kids could see that she had a smile on her face. "Those are our famous Founding Fathers."

Grant frowned. "Well, all I know is that they wore ponytails!" He pointed to a portrait on the wall. Under his breath, he muttered, "Papa would never wear a ponytail."

They all turned to find Papa staring very seriously at a picture on the wall. When they looked, they gasped. It showed a haystack-size mound of amputated arms and legs.

"War is not the best way to solve problems," Papa said sadly. "Back then, there was no anesthesia and no way to save arms and legs shattered by cannon balls. They just cut them off."

Christina looked once then turned away. Grant, of course, got close and examined the picture carefully. "So all wars are bad?"

Papa shook his head. "Sometimes something is important enough to fight to the death for. But most times, it's better to try to talk out your problems and make compromises to solve them."

"Yeah," Grant said. "Like I do with my sister."

Christina slapped her forehead. "Grant, you do not! You never give in. You always..."

"Ok, ok," said Mimi. "This is a battlefield, but no fighting allowed, do you hear me?"

"Yes, Ma'am," said Christina.

"Yeah," said Grant, but behind his back, he gently punched his sister in the side, only he hit her elbow funny bone and she started to laugh uncontrollably. Christina was very ticklish.

Mimi just shook her head. "It must be time for lunch," she told Papa. "The natives are getting restless!"

14 A Surprising New Friend

After a great lunch of chili dogs and chocolate milk, Mimi and Papa surprised their grandchildren by heading back to Jamestown.

"Thank goodness!" Christina whispered to her brother in the back seat.

"You have onion breath," Grant grumbled.

"Do not!" said Christina.

"Do too!" said Grant.

"Please!" said Mimi. "How about a little peace and quiet back there. If you want to 'talk,' maybe you can use your notepad?"

Christina and Grant nodded eagerly. If they used the pad, they could say things that they could not say with their grandparents listening in the front seat.

Christina reopened the notepad and drew little pieces of paper. Each had a question mark on it.

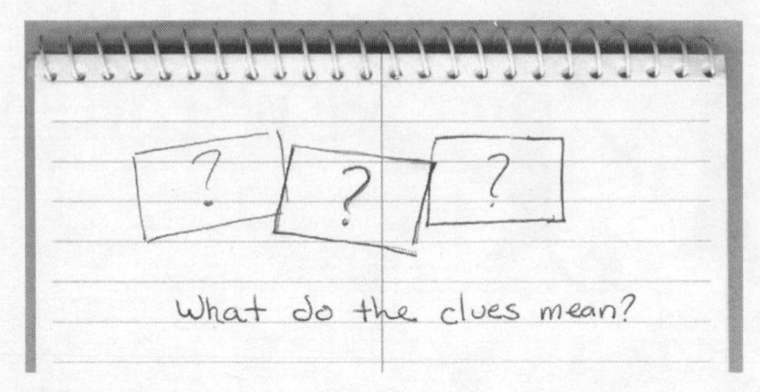

Then, Grant took the pen and drew a skeleton.

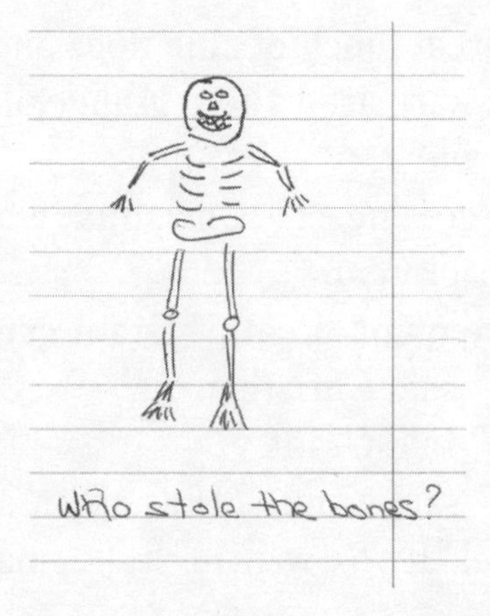

Next, Grant drew a square with little swirls on top.

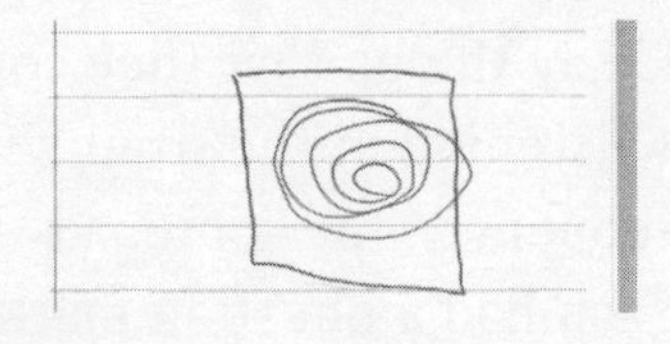

Christina took the pen and wrote...

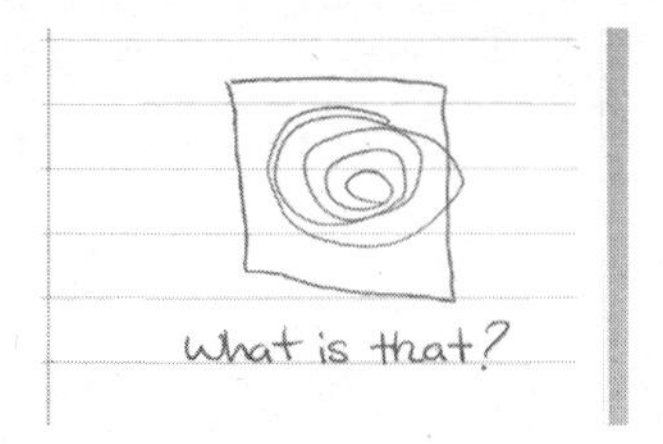

Grant took the pen back and wrote

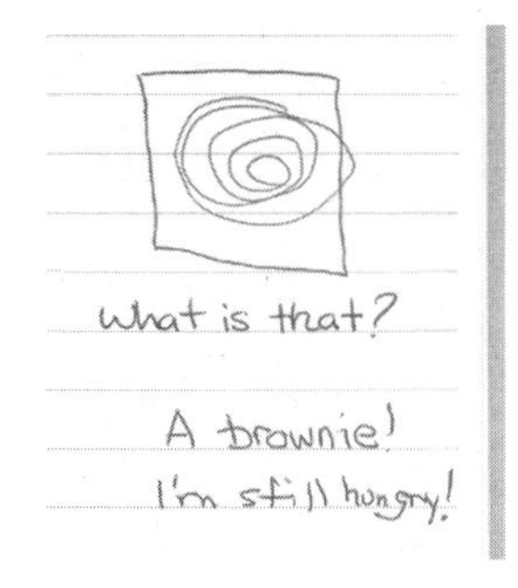

As the kids giggled, they relaxed until they felt Papa swerve the car left and right on the Colonial Parkway. Mimi screamed! Grant and Christina held each other tight as the car tires screeched to a halt.

"What is it, Papa? What's wrong?" Christina begged.

Papa sighed. He turned on the car's flasher lights and got out. "I think I might have hit a dog."

"Oh, no!" said Christina. She and Mimi and Grant craned their necks to see out the car windows. Papa walked in front of the car to the side of the road. He bent over and they all expected the worst.

But suddenly, a brown blur scrambled out of Papa's hands and began to jump up and down on the side of the road.

"Look!" said Christina. "It's a puppy. It's ok!"

"It's so cute," said Mimi. "Thank goodness we didn't hit it."

Outside, Papa scooped up the little dog and got back into the car. "Doggone dog!" he said. "He will get run over for sure if he stays out here. He's just a pup and doesn't know this road is hazardous to his health."

"CAN WE KEEP HIM?! CAN WE KEEP HIM?!!" Christina and Grant squealed together.

"NO!" said Papa.

"NO!" said Mimi.

"But why not?" Christina asked, about to cry. She loved puppies.

"He doesn't belong to anyone," said Grant, hopefully.

"How do you know that?" asked Mimi, puzzled.

"He isn't wearing a collar," said Grant. "Any good dog owner would have a collar and a rabies tag on their dog to show it's had its shots."

"Well, maybe he has a bad owner," Papa said.

"Then we sure can't give him back!" said Christina.

When she saw Mimi and Papa look at one another, Christina cheered: "Yeah! We can keep him!"

"I did not say that, Christina," said Mimi.

"We have to try to find its owner," Papa insisted.

Grant made a big deal out of looking out of all the windows.

"What in the world are you doing, Grant?" asked Mimi.

Grant shrugged his little shoulders. "Looking for the puppy's owner. But I don't see them anywhere. Do you?"

"Ok, ok," said Papa. "We'll take this doggone dog with us as far as Jamestown, so he won't get run over."

"But when we get there, I will put it on the Internet that we found a lost dog," Mimi insisted. "And if someone claims him, we'll have to give him back."

Christina and Grant groaned.

Suddenly, Papa started to laugh. The puppy had climbed up on his neck and was licking him like crazy.

"What kind of silly dog is it, anyway?" asked Mimi. That made the puppy pounce on her and start licking her arms, face, and curls.

In the backseat, Christina and Grant howled with laughter. The dog jumped over the backseat and into their laps. It was a real smoochfest! The puppy slathered them with wet, sloppy kisses...and they did the same to the dog.

"Oh, brother," said Papa. "By the way, it's a bloodhound. That's what kind of dog he is. They're trained to find things or people. They are even used by police or other law enforcement when a crime's been committed."

Christina and Grant got so quiet that Mimi turned around and asked, "What's wrong?"

"Nothing," Christina answered without thinking. "I was just thinking a bloodhound might really come in handy."

Her grandmother looked confused...and suspicious. "Handy for what?" she asked.

Grant came to the rescue. "Handy as a pet!"

15 The Bloodhound

Sure enough, when they got to Jamestown and checked into their motel, Mimi e-mailed an ad to the newspaper for the Lost and Found classifieds. Christina and Grant understood that it was the right thing to do, only they really, really hoped that no one would call and claim "their" puppy.

They could hardly wait to track down Alex and Courtney and find out what was going on, and, to show them the dog, which Papa said they could keep with them on a leash.

After looking for an hour, they finally tracked Courtney down at a concession stand.

"Alex's so upset," she told Grant and Christina. "His dad got out on bail and has a lawyer, but Alex is so ashamed that anyone would believe that his father stole anything at all."

"I can sure understand that," said Christina. "But what about all those clues? Did you guys do any follow-up while we were gone?"

Courtney shook her head. "We tried, but everything came up as a dead end."

"Don't say dead," Grant said.

"Grant! What do you have?" squealed Courtney, as the bloodhound pup bounced out from behind Grant and began to lick Courtney's knees.

"Our new puppy!" Grant said excitedly.

"Grant!" said Christina. "You know that's not true–we found him," she told Courtney, "and we have to wait to see if anyone claims him first. Even then, that doesn't mean that Mimi and Papa will let us keep him."

Courtney scratched the adorable pup behind his ears. "He sure is cute," she said. "What kind of dog is he?"

"A bloodhound!" said Grant. "The kind of dog that tracks scents and finds criminals or lost people or things."

Courtney flushed. "You don't think he could find lost bones, do you?"

Christina frowned. "Maybe if they were lost," she said. "But if they were stolen bones, well, they're probably long gone from here."

"Besides," said Grant, trying hard to hold the active puppy tight on the leash, "he's just a pup. I think they have to be trained to sniff things out, you know."

Just then, Alex dashed up to them. "Hey, you guys!" he yelled as he approached them.

"Thank goodness!" Courtney said to Christina. "I haven't seen Alex much since you guys left for Williamsburg. I've been worried about him."

"Hey, Alex, what's up?" asked Grant, as if it was an ordinary day, instead of a day when a mystery still needed solving, and fast!

Alex waved a piece of white paper at them. "Finally, there's another clue!" he said. "It was tucked in my backpack when I got ready to leave Dad's office this morning. I heard you guys were back and I saw Amy and she said Courtney was at the concession stand, so I tracked you here."

Suddenly, Alex got quiet. Then, he roared, "Speaking of tracking, where'd you get that bloodhound?!"

"You know this breed?" asked Christina, as the puppy ran around in circles, tangling them all up in the leash. As they all laughed, nearby tourists looked too and laughed at the funny scene.

"We found him," Christina explained. "And hope to keep him."

"Well, maybe he can help us!" said Alex. "Read this clue and you'll see what I mean!" He unfolded the note and the other kids–and the dog–gathered around as he read aloud:

"YOUR DAD IS FREE, BUT NOT FOR LONG.
HERE'S ANOTHER CLUE FOR YOU:
IF FINDING THE BONES IS WHAT YOU HOPE,
HEAD FOR THE PLACE WHERE WE GROW SMOKE!"

"Grow smoke?" said Grant. "What does that mean? You can't grow smoke."

Courtney snapped her fingers. "Sure you can," she said. "One of the first successful commercial crops the English settlers learned to grow was tobacco."

"And you smoke tobacco!" said Christina.

"Not if you're smart," said Grant. He squinched up his nose, just imagining the stinky smell of a cigarette or cigar.

"Well, they didn't know 400 years ago that tobacco was so bad for you," said Alex. "And they were desperate to find something to export back to England so they could take the money they got and buy goods they needed or wanted."

"But what in the world does the clue mean?" asked Courtney. "And why did one only show up again as soon as Grant and Christina came back?"

Everyone was silent. These were good questions to which they had no answers.

Courtney had an idea. "There's a demonstration plot of tobacco growing nearby," she said. "John Rolfe was the first colonist to try growing tobacco in the colony."

"You mean the John Rolfe that Pocahontas married?" asked Christina.

"Yes," said Courtney. "But planting and harvesting the crop took lots more workers than they had in the colony, so they began to bring black boys and men from Africa–against their will–to work the fields."

I found a clue!

"You mean they kidnapped them and made them slaves?" asked Grant.

"Sadly true," said Courtney.

They all stood there thinking about this for a moment, then Alex said, "Well, let's at least go look at the tobacco crop and see if it has anything to do with this curious clue."

"Where is it?" asked Christina.

"You know, I forget," said Courtney.

Suddenly, Grant inched the puppy near a man who was smoking a pipe. The dog took a couple of sniffs. "Track that smell," Grant bent low and whispered to the dog.

Christina laughed. "Grant, tobacco plants don't smell like the tobacco used in something like a pipe."

Grant frowned. "This dog is smart!" he insisted. "Look! He's tugging on the leash hard now. Let's follow him and see where he takes us."

And the kids had to, because suddenly, the puppy tore off, pulling Grant along behind him. They followed, racing up and down paths, saying, "Excuse me!" "Sorry!" "Pardon me, please!" as they almost knocked down tourists, young and old.

Soon, they found themselves on the edge of the settlement, and sure enough, right in front of the plot of tobacco plants.

"Told you!" said Grant, although even he was surprised and wondered if the dog was just lucky.

It was then that Christina's cell phone rang in her pocket. Uh, oh, she thought. Was this an emergency? The other kids stared at her as she answered and nodded and gravely shook her head, then said, "Ok, I understand."

When she hung up, they all asked, "What's going on?"

Christina sighed in disappointment. "It was Papa," she said. "He said to come back to the room. Someone showed up about the ad in the newspaper."

16 The Rescuer

As they traipsed forlornly back to the motel, the kids took turns walking the puppy, petting him, and feeding him dog biscuits from Grant's pocket.

Papa was waiting for them at the door with a grim look on his face. Mimi sat at the desk and would not even look at the children. That made Christina know that it was bad.

An older woman sat on the bed. She held a paper sack in one hand and some papers in the other. When she spotted the puppy, she jumped up and grabbed him. "Oh, thank goodness!" she said over and over. "I was so worried about you. Thank heavens you're safe." The puppy seemed thrilled to be in the woman's arms.

"You have a nice dog," said Grant, sadly.

The woman smiled at him. "Oh, he's not my dog. He was someone's dog, but they left him in the marsh near my house. I handle rescue dogs, so I took him in, only he is so energetic"–at this, the puppy bounced from bed to bed as if to prove to everyone just how energetic he was!–

"that he got off his leash and disappeared. That must be when you found him on the Parkway."

"So he's a rescue dog like those dogs that rescue people buried in the snow?" Christina asked, confused.

"Oh, no," said the woman. "He's a pure bloodhound. The kind of rescue dog I'm talking about is when someone like me finds a dog and rescues him, then tries to find him a good owner."

Christina and Grant beamed. "So could we be his new owners?" they asked together.

"If you want to," said the lady. "You seem like a very nice family. And you did rescue my rescue dog!" she added.

"PAPA...MIMI...MIMI...PAPA...PLEASE!...CAN WE?...PLEASE?...WE'LL TAKE GOOD CARE OF HIM...HE LOVES US!...WE LOVE HIM!...PLEASE... PLEASE?!" Grant and Christina went on and on.

Mimi looked at Papa and Papa looked at Mimi, and when they finally both grinned at one another, Christina and Grant knew that they had a new dog!

"Good for you," said Alex.

"He's a great dog," added Courtney.

Christina looked at the woman, who was handing over the sack and the papers to Mimi. "What's the dog's name?" she asked.

The woman looked at her and shook her head. "I haven't a clue!" she said.

17 Clue!

"Of course!" said Christina.

"Of course!" squealed Grant.

"Of course!" agreed Courtney.

"Of course!" shouted Alex.

Mimi and Papa looked puzzled. So did the woman. "Of course what?" Papa said.

Christina giggled. "Well, of course, a bloodhound who tracks people and things that are missing should be named CLUE!"

Everyone laughed, except Clue, who decided at that moment to hike up his leg and wet Mimi's best pair of shoes! Then he grabbed a pillow off the bed with his teeth and shook and shook and shook until feathers began to fly everywhere!

"He's going to be a handful," said the woman.

"Our grandchildren are a handful," said Mimi, looking sadly at her good shoes.

"He has to be housebroken," said Papa. "And fed. And bathed. And all those doggone things."

"We will! We will!" promised Grant and Christina together.

"Gruuuuff!" said Clue.

When Papa suggested that the kids take Clue outside for a walk, they were very eager. Now that he was their very own bloodhound clue-hunting mystery dog, they were ready to get to work. As quickly as they could, they hurried back to the tobacco patch.

"Ok," said Grant, "what are we supposed to be sniffing out here?"

"The clue doesn't tell us that," said Courtney.

For a few minutes, they walked up and down the rows of green-eared tobacco leaves.

"It's hard to believe something this pretty ends up as stinky old cigarettes," said Christina.

"Or snuff!" said Courtney.

"Let's look for bones, please," pleaded Alex.

For awhile, they saw nothing suspicious, until they reached the last plant on the final row. There, attached to a stalk with gardening twine, was another white note.

Alex reached it first. "Beat you, Clue," he said to the puppy, which nipped at his heels in chase.

"Another clue?" groaned Christina. "I thought for sure we'd find something besides another clue. I feel like we're just going around in circles."

"Well, let's at least see what it says," Courtney suggested.

Alex unfolded the paper and the children read:

"SO YOU THINK A DUMB DOG CAN HELP YOU?
DID YOU FORGET JAMES FORT?
WHAT KIND OF MYSTERY-SOLVERS ARE YOU?"

"Hmm," said Courtney, looking all around behind them. "I feel like someone is watching us closely."

"But are they really trying to help us solve the mystery...or leading us on a wild goose chase?" added Christina.

"Good question," said Grant, "but they are right: we skipped right over the Fort James clue when we were gone. So maybe it's not to late to go there."

"But there is no Fort James," Alex surprised them by saying. "I mean there was, but now all we've found is some of the outline of the footprint of the fort."

"What else do you know about the fort?" asked Christina.

"Well, it was triangular in shape...it was a wooden palisade. You know," Alex said, when the others looked puzzled, "the walls were small trees cut to a point on top and all butted together. Inside there were buildings made of wattle-and-daub with thatched roofs."

"What's...what's that stuff you just said?" asked Grant.

"Wattle-and-daub," said Courtney. "It's a mixture of mud and straw they made house walls from."

"So if we can't see the fort, how can we go to the fort?" asked Christina in frustration.

Suddenly, Alex snapped his fingers. "We need to go back to the Archaearium! There are some special effects there that show where the fort was and what it looked like."

"So we can use high tech to see the past?" asked Christina.

"You bet," said Alex.

"It's like returning to the scene of the crime," said Courtney. "Isn't that supposed to be a good thing to do in a mystery? Or is it a bad thing?"

"It's the only thing," said Christina. "We are running out of options and out of time!"

18 Out of Options, Out of Time

Clue led the way as if he knew exactly where he was going. Grant had to hold on tight just to keep up. The others followed behind as fast as they could.

Huffing and puffing, they barely squeaked into the Archaearium with the last tour of the day.

"No getting locked in this time, ok?" said Grant.

"Oh, I don't know," whispered Christina. "Frankly, I'd like to have a look around this place by ourselves with no one else around."

Suddenly, one of the archaeologists turned Grant right around. "You can't bring a dog in here!" he said. "Not unless it's a seeing eye dog."

"You guys go ahead," said Grant. He was not turning Clue loose. "We'll look around out here."

The other kids nodded and went inside. Grant headed back outside and let Clue nose around the building.

"Hey, kid," a man called to Grant. "Would you take this over to the mail station for me?"

Grant spun around to see a man in dirty overalls who wore a slouch hat so far down over his face that Grant couldn't see him well. However, he did notice that the man wore the dirtiest work boots he had ever seen. Dried mud was caked in all the laces.

When Grant answered, "Sure," and reached out for the package, he was shocked to hear Clue begin to growl. When Grant took the package, Clue barked and snapped at the muddy laces.

"Whoa, Clue," said Grant. "It's ok; those are just some dirty shoes."

"Thanks, kid," the man said and skulked away.

"Sure," said Grant, but suddenly he did not feel so sure of himself. Hadn't they started this mystery by going to the mail station? It just seemed too suspicious.

Grant looked hard for the other kids to come out of the Archaearium, but they did not. Finally, he got impatient, and besides, Clue was tugging on his leash. "We'll just go deliver this package and come right back," he said to the puppy. "Our good deed for the day."

Quickly, Grant and Clue started down the path toward the mail station. The faster Clue pulled, the faster Grant had to walk, then run. As he ran, he heard the contents of the box rattle...rattle like bones!

Just before he got to the mail station, Grant tugged Clue off the path and into the trees. "Here, Clue, sniff this, boy." Clue happily sniffed and slobbered all over the hastily wrapped package tied up with string. Clue then began to growl.

This made Grant worry that perhaps the man had followed him. He looked all around, and when his back was turned to the forest, he felt a hand reach out and grab him by the shoulder. He yelped! Clue barked!

19 Big Trouble!

Grant spun around and was shocked, yet relieved, to see the other kids. "Are you trying to scare me?"

"No," said Christina. "We just couldn't find anything helpful at the Archaearium so we took a shortcut Alex knows through the woods." Then she whispered to her brother, "It made him too upset to be at the Archaearium when they had his dad's office all closed up with yellow crime tape."

"Oh," said Grant.

"And someone told us they saw you and Clue and you had a package and were heading toward the mail station," said Courtney. "What gives?"

Grant explained about the man and showed them the package.

"That's just entirely too suspicious," said Christina. "Let me read the address it's going to."

Grant turned the package around and they all looked at the mailing label:

OCCUPANT
POST OFFICE BOX 101A
RICHMOND, VIRGINIA

"That's weird," said Grant. "Someone lives in a post office box?"

Courtney giggled. "No, silly," she said. "That's just where he gets his mail."

"Listen!" said Grant, and he shook the package hard.

"Wow!" said Christina. "If anything ever sounded like rattling bones, it's that."

Alex snatched the package away. "We're going to open it and see!"

"No!" said Courtney. "That's against the law; we'll all go to jail."

"Well, so will my dad for a long time if we don't solve this mystery," Alex argued.

"Everyone who votes to open the package, raise your right hand," said Christina.

Alex and Courtney raised their hands; Christina and Grant did not. Then, amazingly, Clue "ruffff'd" and stuck up one paw.

"I guess that breaks the tie," Alex insisted and began to tear into the package. Sure enough, when he got it open, it contained bones–dog bones! Clue was the only one who was happy.

A suspicious package

"Now why would anyone mail dog bones through the mail?" asked Christina. "Could this be another red herring?"

"It makes no sense at all," said Courtney.

Suddenly, the man who had given Grant the package came storming out of the woods behind them. "Hey, kid!" he screamed. "I thought I told you to mail that package!" He grabbed the box away and the bones clattered to the ground.

Clue growled loudly. The man kicked at the dog.

"No!" said Grant. "Don't kick our dog!"

"You kids are in big trouble!" the man snarled.

Suddenly, Christina grabbed up one of the bones. "No," she said. "I think YOU are in big trouble, buddy."

The other kids didn't understand. Then they looked closely at the bone and realized that it was not a dog bone at all, but a different kind of bone.

The man grabbed for the bone with one hand and for any kid he could reach with the other. As he tried to fight them, Grant tugged the man's slouch hat down over his face. While the man could not see, Alex reached down and tied the man's muddy shoelaces together. The next time he tried to kick Clue, he fell back onto the ground and could not get up.

As the kids scrambled to get out of his way, they heard a loud whistle behind them. It was the police! "Stop! Freeze!" the policeman cried.

The kids weren't sure who he meant, so they did indeed stop in their tracks: Alex on the ground on his stomach; Courtney with a rock in her hand; Grant holding the opened mail parcel; and Christina, holding a human bone in her hand!

And then, to make things worse, Mimi and Papa made an appearance. Even Clue got down on his belly and whimpered. They were indeed all in BIG TROUBLE!

20 Captain John Smith to the Rescue!

"Who are you?" the policeman asked Mimi and Papa.

"We are Mimi and Papa," Mimi said. "We are two of these children's grandparents. Who are you?"

"I'm Captain John Smith," said the policeman. "And I've been on the lookout for HIM!" He pointed to the man on the ground.

"And who is he?" asked Papa.

"He's the man who stole the bones!" blurted Grant.

"And is this his dog?" asked the policeman.

"NO!" said Grant and Christina together. "He's ours!"

"I know you," said the policeman, pointing to Courtney. "You're Amy's sister."

"And YOU," he said to Alex. "You belong to Joe."

By now, Christina had stood still for so long that her arms and legs hurt. "And who," she asked, with a quiver in her voice, "is THIS, please?" She held the human bone aloft a little higher, in hopes someone would take it from her.

And someone did–CLUE!–who scampered off into the woods with one of the most valuable leg bones in the world!

21 Them Bones, Them Bones, Them Dry Bones

Quickly, Captain John Smith slapped handcuffs on the man on the ground. Then he blew his whistle over and over as he chased Clue into the woods.

Grant chased after them. Then Christina. Then Courtney and Alex. Then Mimi and Papa. Soon they were all out of breath and could hardly take another step when they came upon Clue digging madly in the dirt. As they all came to the edge of the hole, they looked down and were shocked to see: SKELETAL REMAINS!

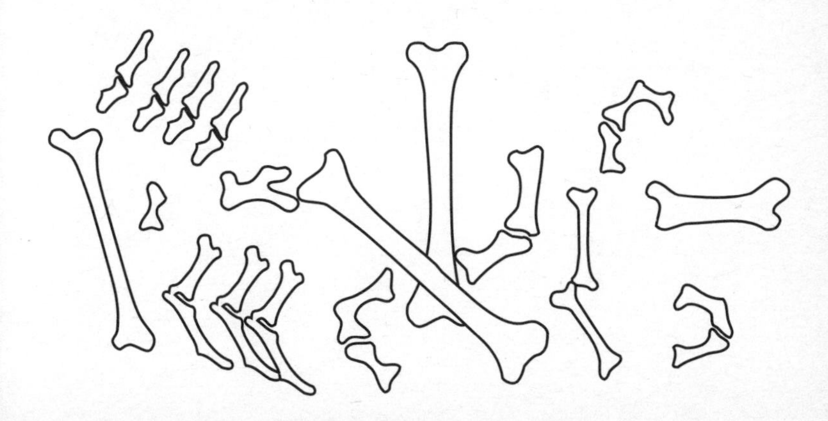

"I don't know who that bone you had belonged to, young lady," said Captain Smith, "but I believe that we just found the rest of him!"

A shocking discovery

22 And a Good Time Was Had by All!

Several hours later, Mimi, Papa, Christina, Grant, Amy, Courtney, Alex, and Joe sat on the deck of a waterside restaurant overlooking Jamestown. It was a celebration dinner!

"I just want to thank you all for working so hard on my behalf," Joe said. He raised his glass of iced tea in a toast to them all, including Clue, who thumped his tail happily on the deck.

"You know," Mimi said, adjusting her wide-brimmed straw hat with the red and white ribbon trim, "I just don't know how you two kids can get into so much mystery trouble when I think I am keeping such a good eye on you!"

Christina and Grant giggled.

"Well, Mimi, if it's any consolation, you almost thwarted our search for clues when you took us to Williamsburg and Yorktown," Christina confessed.

"Yeah, but we would never have found good, old, Clue if we hadn't taken those side trips!" said Grant. He grabbed Clue around the neck in a big hug and fed him a hush puppy from the bread basket on the table.

Papa frowned. "Yeah," he said, "we sure are glad we made that side trip." When everyone looked at him, he broke into a grin. He already loved Clue as much as they all did.

"What I don't understand," said Amy, with a serious look at Courtney, "is why you kids didn't think to come and ask us adults for help."

Courtney sighed. "I guess we got caught up in the moment. We just kept thinking we were so close to solving the mystery and saving Joe's job and reputation, that we just kept going."

"I think it's the bad guy who got caught!" said Grant happily. "He was one scary dude!"

"Yeah," Alex chimed in. "And to think he used to be one of my dad's best workers. He sure did try to trick us with all those red herring clues."

"I think he was just trying to be *duplicitous*," said Mimi.

"Do what?" asked Grant.

"I mean I think he hoped to keep you out of his hair while he stole those valuable artifacts...but then he also used you kids to help do his dirty work mailing the packages so he wouldn't be seen doing it himself."

"It was a pretty nifty scam," Joe admitted. "He had too much knowledge and too much access and too few scruples. Selling black market historical artifacts has tempted people way back to the pyramids in Ancient Egypt.

You can get a lot of money for artifacts from collectors who turn a blind eye to where the treasures come from."

"But all that kind of stuff belongs to us, doesn't it?" asked Christina. "I mean it's our history."

"That's the way I feel," said Joe. "Finding all these skeletal remains is helping us complete the history of America's birth 400 years ago. It's like a big puzzle, and it doesn't help if someone steals or destroys the pieces!"

"Good thing about Captain John Smith coming along just in the nick of time," said Courtney. "He said all the stolen bones had been recovered either in that box, buried in the forest, or being held in the post office box in Richmond."

"Yes," said Joe, taking a big swig of tea, "I have two things to thank you kids for–keeping me out of jail and finding the bones before they disappeared forever."

"And don't forget to thank Clue!" said Grant. "He's gonna be a great bloodhound and tracker. Mimi, I'll bet he can help you in all our mysteries."

Mimi rared back. "OUR mysteries? OUR mysteries?!" Then she laughed. "I guess they are all our mysteries now," she said. "I'm counting on you, too, Clue," she said to the squirming puppy. "Hmm, I wonder if dog food is tax deductible?"

Everyone laughed, then grew quiet at the thought of part of America's precious history vanishing for all time. As the sun began to set on the James River, they looked out at the waters where those colonists had first seen their new home.

"I just have to ask one more question," said Grant with a blush. When everyone looked at him, he said, "You know that Captain John Smith policeman? Well, he's not the same dude who sailed that ship over here 400 years..."

Before Grant could finish his sentence, everyone began to laugh joyfully. Grant grinned sheepishly, hoping they knew he'd just been teasing.

Christina smiled. She liked her history happy. Just like this!

THE END

I wonder what the
next mystery will be...
I don't have a clue!
Clue

ABOUT THE SERIES CREATOR

Carole Marsh is an author and publisher who has written many works of fiction and non-fiction for young readers. She travels throughout the United States and around the world to research her books. In 1979 Carole Marsh was named Communicator of the Year for her corporate communications work with major national and international corporations.

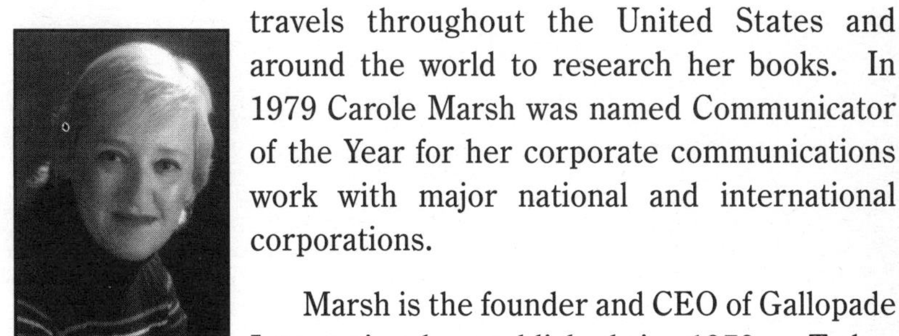

Marsh is the founder and CEO of Gallopade International, established in 1979. Today, Gallopade International is widely recognized as a leading source of educational materials for every state and many countries. Marsh and Gallopade were recipients of the 2002 Teachers' Choice Award. Marsh has written more than 13 Carole Marsh Mysteries™. Years ago, her children, Michele and Michael, were the original characters in her mystery books. Today, they continue the Carole Marsh Books tradition by working at Gallopade. By adding grandchildren Grant and Christina as new mystery characters, she has continued the tradition for a third generation.

Ms. Marsh welcomes correspondence from her readers. You can e-mail her at carole@gallopade.com, visit the carolemarshmysteries.com website, or write to her in care of Gallopade International, P.O. Box 2779, Peachtree City, Georgia, 30269 USA.

Built-In Book Club
Talk About It!

1. Would you like to tag along with Mimi, Papa, Christina, Grant, and Clue on one of their mystery adventures? Why or why not?

2. Why do you think the author, Carole Marsh, picked this particular setting for a story?

3. What did you learn about the founding of Jamestown that you did not know?

4. What do archaeologists do? Would you like to be an archaeologist?

5. Why would people steal historic artifacts? What might they do with them? Are collectors who buy "stolen" artifacts equally guilty of stealing, in your opinion?

6. Who does history belong to? Why should we study history? What is history? When will "today" become "history"?

7. Were you surprised when Papa discovered the bloodhound puppy? What is a "rescue" dog? What kind of dog would you like to "rescue"?

8. What part does cooperation play in the mystery? Creative thinking?

9. What is a "red herring" in a mystery story?

10. How does dialogue move the action along in this mystery?

11. What do you think that the author wrote that was "real"? What do you think she made up?

12. Have you heard of The Lost Colony? Plymouth Rock? What do these events, along with Jamestown, tell you about how America was founded? Hint: Try, try again?!

Built-In Book Club
Bring It To Life

1. Color the Jamestown mural, if you got this in your Jamestown Mystery Set. Otherwise, get a large piece of kraft paper and draw a mural of Jamestown with the three ships, the Powhatan Indian village, Archaearium, and more.

2. Make fried hominy! Buy canned hominy in the grocery store. You can coat it in corn meal if you wish. Fry it in a frying pan in a little butter until golden brown. Serve warm with some wildwood honey!

3. Write a play based on this mystery! There are many characters in the book you can play. Select certain dialogue to "speak." make simple sets and props. Make simple costumes, even if that is just hats and other props. Perform your play for another class, on parent night, or for the school!

4. Research Native American Indian games such as "Kick Stick," "Guard the Chief," and "Rattler" and try playing them yourselves!

5. Write a story about what could have happened if the Jamestown colony had failed...what would have happened to "America?"

Glossary

artifact: object made and used by people in the past

GPS: Global Positioning System; a network of satellites that can tell your exact location

industrious: working hard and in a steady way

options: choices

pun: a word or phrase that can have two meanings, one usually funny, even though it may not have been intended to be funny

reputation: what people think about the character of a person or thing

ruse: a sneaky trick

scruples: morals or values

VIP: Very Important Person or Very Important People

SCAVENGER HUNT!

Recipe for fun: Read the book, take the tour, find the items on this list and check them off! (Hint: Look high and low!!) *Teachers: you have permission to reproduce this form for your students.*

___1. Picture of Captain John Smith, the colonist, not the policeman!

___2. Picture of Pocahontas–it may surprise you!

___3. Definition of the term "Archaearium."

___4. Corn on the cob (the colonists ate a lot of it once they were able to grow it!)

___5. Picture of a bloodhound–check out that nose!

___6. One of these tools that might be used by an archaeologist:
trowel (for gentle digging)
paintbrush (for brushing away dirt)
measuring tape (to measure artifacts)

___7. Compass rose (or a picture of one)

___8. Something that could be used to make wattle and daub!

JAMESTOWN

Places To Go
& Things To Know!

Visit these two sites to get the scoop on what's happening to celebrate Jamestown's 400th anniversary:

http://www.americas400thanniversary.com/
http://www.jamestown2007.org/home.cfm

What are archaeologists finding at the original site of Jamestown? Check out all the exciting discoveries at:

http://www.historicjamestowne.org/ and
http://www.apva.org/jr.html

Learn how the colonists really lived at the Jamestown Settlement living history museum and exhibits, and explore the Yorktown Victory Center:

http://www.historyisfun.org/

Want to know more about Pocahontas? Check out:

http://www.apva.org/history/pocahont.html

You can read more about Captain John Smith at:

http://www.apva.org/history/jsmith.html

Mysteries of Jamestown and amazing "secrets of the dead" unfold at the Public Broadcasting System website:

http://www.pbs.org/wnet/secrets/case_jamestown/

Learn all about Colonial Williamsburg at:

http://www.history.org/

Want to make your own tricorn hat? Find directions at:

www.cvesd.k12.ca.us/finney/paulvm/PR3_TricornHat.pdf

Visit *www.bloodhound.org* to learn more about this pretty amazing breed!

Visit *www.carolemarshmysteries.com* for lots of fun activities!

Enjoy this exciting excerpt from

THE MYSTERY ON THE FREEDOM TRAIL

1 WHAT IN THE WORLD IS A BM ANYWAY?

"Boston is a long way from Georgia," Christina mused as she read the curious white note with the red lining once again. "I guess we'd have to take an airplane."

Christina Yother, 9, a fourth-grader in Peachtree City, Georgia, her brother, Grant, 7, and their Grandmother Mimi stood around the bright red mailbox. They ignored the bills, advertisements, and the little box of free detergent stuffed in the mailbox to concentrate on the invitation to visit Boston. The invitation read:

Mimi,

You and your two delightful grandchildren are invited to visit us during the big BM! Cousins Derian and C.F. will enjoy showing the kids Bean Town! Let me know ASAP. Patriots' Day is coming soon, you know!

Love,
Emma

Mimi tapped the note with her bright red fingernail. "I guess Patriots' Day *is* coming soon. Today is the last day of March. She could have given us a little more notice."

Of course, Christina knew that didn't really matter to her Grandmother Mimi. She was not like most grandmothers. She wasn't really like a grandmother at all. She had bright blond hair, wore all the latest sparkly clothes, was the CEO of her own company, and took off for parts unknown at a moment's notice.

"Aunt Emma sure likes exclamation points," observed Christina. "Just like you, Mimi!"

"You bet!" said Mimi, giving her granddaughter's silky, chestnut-colored hair a tousle. "I'm the Exclamation Mark Queen!" She looked down at Grant who was fingering the corner of the invitation. He looked very serious. "What's wrong, Grant?" asked Mimi.

Even standing on the curb, Grant was small. His blue eyes seemed the biggest part of him. He looked up at his grandmother. "Well, for one thing, Aunt Emma sure uses a lot of letters instead of words. What does ASAP stand for?"

Christina knew that one. (Of course, she always did!) "It means As Soon As Possible–right, Mimi?"

"That's right," said Mimi. "You can say A-S-A-P, or say it like a word–asap."

"Then I hate to be a sap and ask the next question," said Grant with a sigh.

"What's that?" asked Mimi. "There are no dumb questions, you know."

Grant slid off the curb, looking littler than ever. "It's not the question that bothers me . . . it's the possible answer. I mean what *is* a big BM?"

Mimi laughed. "Not what you apparently think it means! The BM is the Boston Marathon. It's the biggest deal in Boston each year. People come from all over the world to run in this race."

"Oh," Grant said with a grin. He looked relieved, and so did his sister. "So it's like the Peachtree Road Race on the 4th of July?"

"Sort of," said Mimi, folding the note and stuffing it back in its envelope. "Only the Boston Marathon is the oldest marathon in America, so it's really special. It has an incredible history!"

Christina and Grant grabbed one another and groaned. Oh, no! When Mimi said the word *history*, they knew they would be in for a big, long tale of everything about everything. But not this time. She ignored her grandkids' dramatic groaning and headed up the driveway for the house.

Christina chased her, running beneath the overhang of magnolia limbs over the azalea-lined path of pink and purple blooms. "Are we going?"

Grant chased Christina. "Wait up, you two!" he pleaded. He took a shortcut across the wide green lawn, weaving (against Mimi's rules) through the forest of pampas grass spewing fountains of white, feathery spikes. "Are we going?" he begged.

On the front porch, Mimi plopped down in the big, white Victorian rocking chair. She pulled out her cell phone from her jacket pocket. Grant and Christina piled into the rocker beside her. "Are we? Are we?!" they hissed, as Mimi dialed the number. They held their breath until they heard her say, "Emma? We're coming to the Big BM!"

After Mimi hung up the phone, she jiggled the other rocking chair, causing the two kids to giggle. "What's wrong, Grant?" she asked. "You still don't look happy!"

Grant looked at his grandmother thoughtfully. "If we go to Boston, do we get to eat anything beside beans?"

Enjoy this exciting excerpt from

The Mystery at Big Ben

1 Getting There is Half the Fun!

"*BONG! BONG!*" cried Grant. "*BONG... BONG... BONG... BONG!*"

"Grant, if you *bong* one more time, I'm going to *bong* you on the head," his grandmother Mimi said.

They were standing in the middle of busy Heathrow Airport watching for Papa and Grant's sister Christina to appear with the luggage. They had just flown in from Paris aboard Papa's little red and white airplane, *The Mystery Girl.*

Suddenly, an overflowing luggage cart appeared. It staggered left and right toward them as if propelled by a seasick ghost.

Grant jumped just before the cart ran over his foot. “Hey, careful there!” he screeched.

A head thrust out from each side of the cart. “I can’t believe we have so much luggage,” Papa said. He looked handsome in the cowboy hat and boots and leather vest he always wore, but he was panting like a dog.

Christina plopped down on the floor. “This luggage cart is crazy. I thought we’d never get this stuff pushed all the way over here. I’m exhausted!”

“*BONG! BONG! BONG!*” cried Grant yet again.

Christina and Papa stared at him like he was crazy. “And just what is that all about?” Papa asked, holding his head with both hands.

Mimi sighed. “Grant thinks he will just die if we don’t go see Big Ben right away,” she explained. “I do not know why he is so excited about a clock.”

Grant thrust his hands on his hips in his don’t-make-fun-of-me-just-cause-I’m-only-seven pose. “It isn’t just any old clock,” he said. “Big Ben is the most famous clock in the world. It’s tall and it’s loud and I want to see it.”

“I doubt that it’s as loud as you,” Christina teased her brother. She brushed her bangs away from her forehead.

"I doubt anything's as loud as Grant," Papa agreed.

"He's loud, but he's cute and sweet," Mimi said, tousling Grant's blond crewcut, "but I'm still going to *bong* him on the head if he imitates Big Ben anymore till we go and see it for ourselves."

"*Bong...bong...*" whispered Grant.

"What's that?" Christina asked.

"LITTLE BEN!" Grant cried and laughed.

Papa ended the discussion by saying, "Here, pard'ner!" and dumping a large duffle bag into Grant's arms.

"*Ufgh!*" said Grant, swaying under the weight. He wandered left and right. All you could see was the bag and his little arms holding on for dear life and his legs quivering beneath him.

Christina laughed until Papa said, "You, too, Missy!" and tossed her a suitcase that seemed to weigh a ton.

"These are too heavy!" Christina complained.

"Then next time don't pack so much," said Papa. "Those are *your* bags, you know." Papa threw a hanging bag over his shoulder and picked up a small case. "And these are mine," he said with a smile.

Grant had dropped his duffle to the floor.

Christina did the same. "Then whose are all those?!" they asked, pointing to a large mound of bright red suitcases of all sizes.

Papa looked at Mimi. Christina looked at Mimi. Grant looked at Mimi. Mimi looked at the ceiling ignoring them all.

"Mimi!" Christina squealed. "What is all that stuff?"

Mimi looked at them and smiled secretively. "Oh, you know. This and that. I do have to meet the Queen, you know. And I have to write a mystery, you know. So, you know, I need a lot of stuff."

Papa just shook his head tiredly. Christina and Grant laughed. Mimi wrote mystery books for kids and set them in real locations, like the one she would be working on here in London, England. Papa was "travel agent" and "trail boss." And when Christina and Grant were out of school, they got to tag along, and were supposed to stay out of the way... but they never did! Why? Because they felt it was their official job to help Mimi discover mysterious facts and places and people to put in her books.

But sometimes, things backfired. Like now? For suddenly, there was a loud BOOM which echoed throughout the busy terminal.

"What was that?" said Mimi.

"Was it a bomb?" Christina asked. She knew there had been some terrorist bombs in London in the past.

"No!" said Grant. "It's that!"

They all turned around and stared at the overloaded luggage cart which had tipped and fallen over, tossing all of Mimi's red luggage to the floor.

"*Ufgh!*" said Papa with a sigh and began to hoist all the suitcases back into place.

WRITE YOUR OWN REAL KIDS REAL PLACES MYSTERY!

Make up a dramatic title!

You can pick four real kid characters!

Select a real place for the story's setting!

Try writing your first draft!

Edit your first draft!

Read your final draft aloud!

You can add art, photos or illustrations!

Share your book with others and send me a copy!

Six Secret Writing Tips from Carole Marsh!

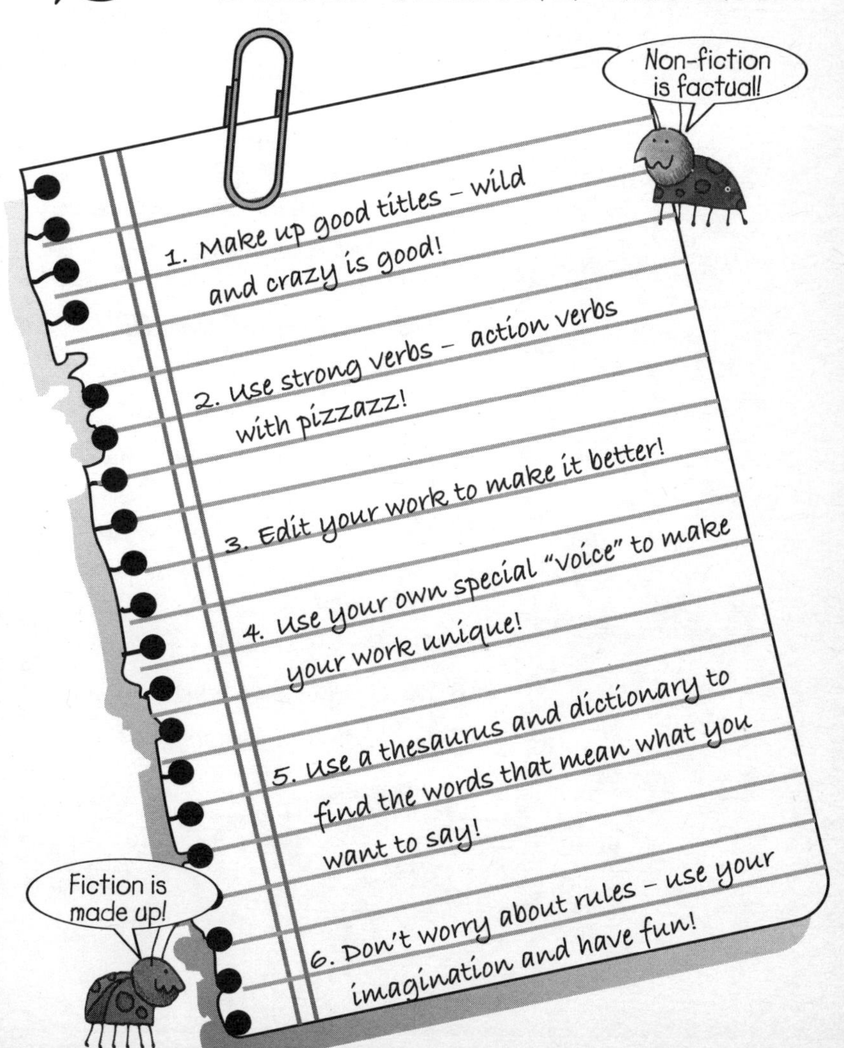

The Carole Marsh Mysteries Series

- #1 *The Mystery of Biltmore House*
- #2 *The Mystery on the Freedom Trail*
- #3 *The Mystery of Blackbeard the Pirate*
- #4 *The Mystery of the Alamo Ghost*
- #5 *The Mystery on the California Mission Trail*
- #6 *The Mystery of the Chicago Dinosaurs*
- #7 *The White House Christmas Mystery*
- #8 *The Mystery on Alaska's Iditarod Trail*
- #9 *The Mystery at Kill Devil Hills*
- #10 *The Mystery in New York City*
- #11 *The Mystery at Disney World*
- #12 *The Mystery on the Underground Railroad*
- #13 *The Mystery in the Rocky Mountains*
- #14 *The Mystery on the Mighty Mississippi*
- #15 *The Mystery at the Kentucky Derby*
- #16 *The Ghost of the Grand Canyon*
- #17 *The Mystery at Jamestown*

CAROLE MARSH MYSTERIES™

WOULD YOU LIKE TO BE A CHARACTER IN A CAROLE MARSH MYSTERY?

If you would like to star in a Carole Marsh Mystery, fill out the form below and write a 25-word paragraph about why you think you would make a good character! Once you're done, ask your mom or dad to send this page to:

Carole Marsh Mysteries Fan Club
Gallopade International
P.O. Box 2779
Peachtree City, GA 30269

My name is: ______________________________

I am a: ____boy ____ girl Age: ______________

I live at: ______________________________

City: ______________ State:____ Zip code: ________

My e-mail address: ______________________________

My phone number is: ______________________________

____

____

____

____

____

____

____

____

____

____

A NEW PET!

Christina and Grant have a new pet, Clue. They are so excited! They would like for you to share a picture of you and your pet with them.

Mail pictures to:
Carole Marsh Mysteries
PO Box 2779
Peachtree City, GA 30269

Or, email pictures to:
funstuff@gallopade.com

Be sure to tell us your name and age, and your pet's name and age.

Christina and Grant will be checking the mail every day!

VISIT THE CAROLE MARSH MYSTERIES WEBSITE

www.carolemarshmysteries.com

- *Check out what's coming up next! Are we coming to your area with our next book release? Maybe you can have your book signed by the author!*
- *Join the Carole Marsh Mysteries Fan Club!*
- *Apply for the chance to be a character in an upcoming Carole Marsh Mystery!*
- *Learn how to write your own mystery!*